It was her. He knew it was her.

The honey-blond hair was longer and pulled into a ponytail, but it was her. He felt, more than visualized her, and his body quickened in response even after all these months.

Then she turned and presented her profile, and he felt every ounce of blood drain from his face.

What the ever-loving hell?

There was no mistaking the full curve of her belly.

Kelly was pregnant. *Very* pregnant.

Dread took hold of his throat and squeezed until his nostrils twitched with the effort of drawing air.

There was a possibility it was his child.

Or his brother's.

Dear Reader,

I love when a story grabs me by the throat and has so much emotion and angst in it that I get that knot, and it just stays there as I hold my breath waiting to see how the hero and heroine are going to make it past seemingly insurmountable obstacles.

Wanted by Her Lost Love was just such a story for me. I wrote it with an ache in my chest because I hurt for both Kelly and Ryan and I was anxious to give them the happily ever after they deserve.

So much of their story is about moving past mistakes and learning to forgive. But mostly it's about a heroine who stands up for herself and decides that she deserves more after she's been badly misjudged and mistreated by the people around her. Her emotional journey is one of my favorites and I hope you're rooting for her right alongside me as you turn the pages.

Maya Banks

Wanted by Her Lost Love

MAYA BANKS

First published in Great Britain 2012
by Mills & Boon, an imprint of Harlequin (UK) Limited.
Large Print edition 2012
Harlequin (UK) Limited,
Eton House, 18-24 Paradise Road,
Richmond, Surrey TW9 1SR

ISBN: 978 0 263 22972 1

Harlequin (UK) policy is to use papers that are natural, renewable and recyclable products and made from wood grown in sustainable forests. The logging and manufacturing process conform to the legal environmental regulations of the country of origin.

Printed and bound in Great Britain
by CPI Antony Rowe, Chippenham, Wiltshire

MAYA BANKS

has loved romance novels from a very (very) early age, and almost from the start, she dreamed of writing them, as well. In her teens she filled countless notebooks with overdramatic stories of love and passion. Today her stories are only slightly less dramatic, but no less romantic.

She lives in Texas with her husband and three children and wouldn't contemplate living anywhere other than the South. When she's not writing, she's usually hunting, fishing or playing poker. She loves to hear from her readers, and she can be found on Facebook (www.facebook.com/pages/Maya-Banks/323801453301?ref=ts) or you can follow her on Twitter (www.twitter.com/maya_banks). Her website, www.mayabanks.com is where you can find up-to-date information on all of Maya's current and forthcoming releases.

To the kidlets
for being so helpful and understanding
when mom has to work

One

"Almost enough to make you believe in the fine institution of marriage, isn't it?" Ryan Beardsley said as he watched his friend, Raphael de Luca, dance with his radiant new bride, Bryony.

The reception was taking place inside Moon Island's small, nondescript municipal building. It wasn't exactly where Ryan imagined any of his friends would host a wedding reception, but he supposed it was fitting that Rafe and Bryony would marry here on the island where so much of their relationship had been forged.

The bride positively glowed, and the swell of her belly added to her beauty. They stood in the middle of the makeshift dance floor, Bryony tucked into Rafe's protective hold, and they were so focused on each other that Ryan doubted the world around them existed. Rafe looked like he'd been handed the universe, and maybe he had.

"They look disgustingly happy," Devon Carter said next to him.

Ryan chuckled and looked up to see Dev holding a glass of wine in one hand, his other shoved into the pocket of his slacks.

"Yeah, they do."

Dev's mouth twisted in annoyance and Ryan chuckled again. Devon himself wasn't very far away from a trip down the aisle, and he wasn't taking it with good grace. Still, he couldn't resist needling his friend.

"Copeland still putting the screws to you?"

"And how," Devon muttered. "He's determined for me to marry Ashley. He won't budge on the deal unless I agree. And now that we've relocated the resort and begun construction, I'm ready to get on with the next step. I don't want him to lose confidence over this blown deal. Problem is, he's insisted on a dating period. He wants Ashley to be comfortable around me. I swear I think the man believes he lives in the eighteen hundreds. Who the hell arranges a marriage for their daughter anymore? And why the hell would you make marriage a condition of business? I can't wrap my head around it."

"There are worse women to marry, I'm sure," Ryan said, thinking of his own narrow escape.

Devon winced in sympathy. "Still no word on Kelly?"

Ryan frowned and shook his head. "No. But I only just started looking. She'll turn up."

"Why are you looking for her, man? Why would you even want to go back down that road? Forget about her. Move on. You're better off without her. You're out of your mind for pursuing this."

Ryan curled his lip and turned to look at his friend. "I have no doubt I'm better off. I'm not looking for her so I can welcome her back into my life."

"Then why did you hire an investigator to find her, for God's sake? You'd be better off letting the past stay in the past. Get over her. Move on."

Ryan was silent for a long moment. It wasn't a question he could entirely answer. How could he explain the burning desire to know where she was? What she was doing. If she was all right. He shouldn't care, damn it. He should forget all about her, but he couldn't.

"I want some answers," he finally muttered. "She never cashed the check I gave her. I'd just like to know that nothing has happened to her."

The excuse sounded lame even to him.

Devon raised an eyebrow and sipped at the expensive wine. "After what she pulled, I'd imagine she's feeling pretty damn stupid. I wouldn't want to show my face either."

Ryan shrugged. "Maybe." But he couldn't shake the feeling that it was something more. Why was he even worried? Why should he care?

Why hadn't she cashed the check?

Why couldn't he get her out of his mind? She haunted him. For six months, he had cursed her, lain awake at night wondering where she was and if she was safe. And he hated that he cared, even though he convinced himself he'd worry about any woman under the same circumstances.

Devon shrugged. "Your time and your dime. Oh, look, there's Cam. Wasn't sure Mr. Reclusive would actually crawl out of that fortress of his for the event."

Cameron Hollingsworth shouldered his way through the crowd, and people instinctively moved to get out of his way. He was tall and broad chested, and he wore power and refinement like most other people wore clothing. The stone set of his demeanor made him unapproachable by most. He could be a mean son of a bitch, but he could usually be counted on to relax around his friends.

The problem was, the only people he counted as friends were Ryan, Devon and Rafe. He didn't have much patience for anyone else.

"Sorry I'm late," Cameron said as he approached the two men. Then he glanced over the dance floor and his gaze stopped when he came to Rafe and Bryony. "How did the ceremony go?"

"Oh, it was lovely," Devon drawled. "All a woman could hope for, I'm guessing. Rafe didn't give a damn as long as the end result was Bryony being his."

Cam emitted a dry chuckle. "Poor bastard. I don't know whether to offer my condolences or my congratulations."

Ryan grinned. "Bryony's a good woman. Rafe's lucky to have her."

Devon nodded and even Cameron smiled, if you could call the tiny lift at the corner of his mouth a true smile. Then Cam turned to Devon, his eyes gleaming with unholy amusement.

"Word is you're not far from taking a trip down the aisle yourself."

Devon muttered a crude expletive and flipped up his middle finger along the side of his wine-glass. "Let's not ruin Rafe's wedding by talking about mine. I'm more interested in knowing whether you were able to acquire the site for the new location of our hotel since Moon Island is now officially a bust."

Cam's eyebrows went up in exaggerated shock. "You doubt me? I'll have you know that twenty prime acres of beachfront property on St. Angelo is now ours. And I got a damn good deal. Better yet, construction will commence as soon as we can move crews in. If we really dig in, we'll come close to hitting our original deadline for the grand opening."

Their gazes automatically went to Rafe, who was still wrapped around his bride. Yeah, the man had caused them a major setback when he pulled the plug on the Moon Island venture, but it was hard for Ryan to get up in arms about it when Rafe looked so damn happy.

Ryan's pocket vibrated, and he reached down to pull his phone out. He was about to hit the ignore button when he saw who was calling. He frowned. "Excuse me, I need to take this."

Cameron and Devon waved him off and returned to their bantering as Ryan hurried out of the building. As soon as he stepped outside, the sea breeze ruffled his hair and the tang of salt filled his nose.

The weather was seasonable but by no means hot. It was about as perfect a day as you could ask for, especially for a wedding on the beach.

He turned to look at the distant waves and brought the phone to his ear.

"Beardsley," he said by way of a terse greeting.

"I think I've found her," his lead investigator said with no preamble.

Ryan tensed, his hand gripping the phone until his fingers went numb. "Where?"

"I haven't had time to send a man to get a visual confirmation yet. I only just got the information in a few minutes ago. I felt strongly enough about her identity to give you a heads-up. I should know more by tomorrow."

"Where?" Ryan demanded again.

"Houston. She's working in a diner there. There was a mix-up originally in her social security number. Her employer reported it wrong. When he put in the correction, she popped on to my radar. I'll have photos and a full report for you by tomorrow afternoon."

Houston. The irony wasn't lost on him. He'd been close to her all this time and never known it.

"No," Ryan interjected. "I'll go. I'm already in Texas. I can be in Houston in a couple of hours."

There was a long silence over the phone. "Sir,

it might not be her. I prefer to get confirmation before you take a needless trip."

"You said it was most likely her," Ryan said impatiently. "If it turns out not to be, I won't hold you responsible."

"Should I hold off my man then?"

Ryan paused, his lips tight, his grip on the phone even tighter. "If it's Kelly, I'll know. If it's not, I'll inform you so you can continue your search. There's no need for you to send anyone down. I'll go myself."

Ryan drove through Westheimer in the blinding rain. His destination was a small café in west Houston where Kelly was waitressing. It shouldn't surprise him. She'd been waitressing in a trendy New York café when they'd met. But the check he'd written her would have prevented her from needing to work for quite some time. He figured she would have returned to school. Even when they'd become engaged, she'd expressed the desire to finish her degree. He hadn't understood it, but he'd supported her decision.

The selfish part of him had wanted her to be completely reliant on him.

Why hadn't she cashed the check?

He had hopped the ferry to Galveston immediately after giving Rafe and Bryony his best wishes. He hadn't told Cam or Dev that he'd found Kelly, just that he had an important business matter to attend to. By the time he'd gotten to Houston it had been late in the evening, so he'd spent a sleepless night in a downtown hotel.

When he'd gotten up this morning, the skies had been gray and overcast and there hadn't been a single break in the rain since he'd left his hotel. At least the weather had been beautiful for Rafe's wedding. By now the happy couple would be off on their honeymoon—someplace where there was an abundance of blue skies.

He glanced over at his GPS and saw he was still several blocks from his destination. To his frustration, he hit every single red light on the way down the busy street. Why he was in a hurry, he didn't know. According to his investigator, she'd worked here for a while. She wasn't going anywhere.

A million questions hovered in his mind, but he knew he wouldn't have the answers to any of them until he confronted her.

A few minutes later he pulled up and parked at the small corner coffee shop that sported a lopsided doughnut sign. He stared at the place in astonishment, trying to imagine Kelly working *here* of all places.

With a shake of his head, he ducked out of the BMW and dashed toward the entrance, shaking the rain from his collar as he stepped under the small awning over the door.

Once inside, he looked around before taking a seat in a booth on the far side of the café. A waitress who was not Kelly came over with a menu and slapped it down on the table in front of him.

"Just coffee," he murmured.

"Suit yourself," she said as she sashayed off to the bar to pour the coffee.

She returned a moment later and put the cup down with enough of a jolt to slosh the dark brew over the rim. With an apologetic smile, she tossed down a napkin.

"If there's anything I can get you, just let me know."

It was on the tip of his tongue to ask her about Kelly when he looked beyond her and saw a waitress with her back to him standing across the room at another table.

He waved his waitress off and honed in on the table across the café. It was her. He knew it was her.

The honey-blond hair was longer and pulled into a ponytail, but it was her. He felt, more than visualized her, and his body quickened in response even after all these months.

Then she turned and presented her profile, and he felt every ounce of blood drain from his face.

What the everloving hell?

There was no mistaking the full curve of her belly.

She was pregnant. *Very* pregnant. Even more pregnant than Bryony by the looks of her.

His gaze lifted just as she turned fully and their eyes met. Shock widened her blue eyes as she stared across the room at him. Recognition was instant, but then why would she have forgotten him any more than he could have forgotten her?

Before he could react, stand, say anything, fury turned those blue orbs ice-cold. Her delicate features tightened and he could see her jaw clench from where he sat.

What the hell did she have to be so angry about?

Her fingers curled into tight balls at her sides, almost as if she'd love nothing better than to deck him. Then, without a word, she turned and stalked toward the kitchen, disappearing behind the swinging door.

His eyes narrowed. Okay, that hadn't gone as he'd imagined. He wasn't sure what he'd expected. A weeping apology? A plea to take her back? He damn sure hadn't expected to find her heavily pregnant, waiting tables in a dive more suited to a high school dropout than someone who was well on her way to graduating with honors from university as Kelly had been.

Pregnant. He took a deep, steadying breath. Just how pregnant was she? She had to be at least seven months. Maybe more.

Dread took hold of his throat and squeezed until his nostrils twitched with the effort of drawing air.

If she was pregnant, seven *months'* pregnant, there was a possibility it was his child.

Or his brother's.

Kelly Christian burst into the kitchen, struggling to untie her apron. She swore under her breath when she fumbled uselessly at the strings. Her hands shook so bad she couldn't even manage this simple of a task.

Finally she yanked hard enough that the material ripped. She all but threw it on the hook where the other waitresses hung their aprons.

Why was he here? She hadn't done a whole lot to cover her tracks. Yes, she'd left New York, and at the time she hadn't known where she'd end up. She hadn't cared. But neither had she done anything to hide. That meant he could have found her at anytime. Why now? After six months, what possible reason could he have for looking for her?

She refused to believe in coincidences. This

wasn't a place Ryan Beardsley would ever just happen to be. Not his speed. His precious family would die before sullying their palates in anything less than a five-star restaurant.

Wow, Kelly, bitter much?

She shook her head, furious with herself for reacting this strongly to the man's presence.

"Hey, Kelly, what's going on?" Nina asked.

Kelly turned to see the other waitress standing in the doorway to the kitchen, her brow creased with concern.

"Close the door," Kelly hissed as she motioned Nina inside.

Nina quickly complied and the door swung shut. "Is everything all right? You don't look good, Kelly. Is it the baby?"

Oh, God, the baby. Ryan would have been blind not to have seen her protruding belly. She had to get out of here.

"No, I'm not well at all," she said, grasping for an explanation. "Tell Ralph I had to leave."

Nina frowned. "He's not going to like it. You know how he is about us missing work. Unless we're missing a limb or vomiting blood, he's not going to be forgiving."

"Then tell him I quit," Kelly muttered as she hurried toward the alley exit. She paused at the rickety door and turned anxiously back to Nina. "Do me a favor, Nina. This is important, okay? If anyone in the diner asks about me—anyone at all—you don't know anything."

Nina's eyes widened. "Kelly, are in you in some kind of trouble?"

Kelly shook her head impatiently. "I'm not in trouble. I swear it. It's…it's my ex. He's a real bastard. I saw him in the diner a minute ago."

Nina's lips tightened and her eyes blazed with indignation. "You go on ahead, hon. I'll take care of things here."

"Bless you," Kelly murmured.

She ducked out the back door of the diner and headed down the alley. Her apartment was only two blocks away. She could go there and figure out what the heck to do next.

She almost stopped halfway there. Why was she running? She had nothing to hide. She'd done nothing wrong. What she *should* have done was march across that diner and bloodied his nose. Instead she was running.

She took the flimsy stairs to her second-story apartment two at a time. When she was inside, she closed the door and leaned heavily against it.

Tears pricked her eyelids and it only made her more furious that she was actually upset over seeing Ryan Beardsley again. No, she didn't want to face him. She never wanted to see him again. *Never* did she want anyone to have the kind of power he had to hurt her. Never again.

Her hands automatically went to her belly, and she rubbed soothingly, not sure who she was trying to comfort more, her baby or herself.

"I was a fool to love him," she whispered. "I was a fool to think I could ever fit in and that his family would accept me."

She jumped when the door behind her vibrated with a knock. Her heart leaped into her throat, and she put a shaky hand to her chest. She stared at the door as if she could see through it.

"Kelly, open the damn door. I know you're in there."

Ryan. God. The very last person she wanted to open the door to.

She put a hand to the wood and leaned forward, unsure of whether she should ignore him or respond.

The force of his second knock bumped her hand, and she snatched it away.

"Go away," she finally shouted. "I have nothing to say to you."

Suddenly the door shuddered and flew open. She took several hasty steps backward, her arms curling protectively over her belly.

He filled the doorway, looking as big and formidable as ever. Nothing had changed except for new lines around his mouth and eyes. His gaze stroked over her, piercing through any protective barriers she thought to construct. He'd always had a way of seeing right to the heart of her. Except when it mattered the most.

Fresh grief flooded through her chest. Damn him. What else could he possibly want to do to hurt her? He'd already destroyed her.

"Get out," she said, proud of how steady her voice sounded. "Get out or I'll call the police. I have nothing to talk to you about. Not now. Not ever."

"That's too bad," Ryan said as he stalked forward, "because I have plenty to talk to *you* about. Starting with whose baby you're pregnant with."

Two

Kelly willed herself not to rage at him. Instead, she looked calmly at him, coolly, while emotions boiled beneath the surface like molten lava ready to erupt. "It's none of your business."

His nostrils flared. "It is if you're carrying my baby."

She crossed her arms over her chest and stared him down. "Now *why* would you think that?"

For a man only too willing to believe she'd slept around, it seemed pretty damn ridiculous that he'd barge into her apartment demanding to know whether or not her baby was his.

"Damn it, Kelly, we were engaged. We lived

together and were intimate often. I have a right to know if this is my child."

She raised an eyebrow and studied him for a moment. "There is no way to know. After all I was with so *many* other men, your brother included." She shrugged nonchalantly and turned away from him, going into the kitchen.

He was close on her heels and she could feel the anger emanating from him. "You're a bitch, Kelly. A cold, calculating bitch. I gave you everything and you threw it away for a little gratuitous sex on the side."

She whipped around, the urge to hit him so strong that she had to curl her fingers into a fist to keep from doing just that. "Get out. Get out and don't ever come back."

His eyes glittered with anger and frustration. "I'm not going anywhere, Kelly, not until you tell me what I want to know."

She bared her teeth. "It's not your baby. Happy? Now go."

"Is it Jarrod's then?"

"Why don't you ask him?"

"We don't talk about you," he bit out.

"Well, I don't want to talk about *either* of you. I want you out of my apartment. It isn't your baby. Get out of my life. I did as you asked. I got out of yours."

"You didn't give me a choice."

She looked scornfully at him. "Choice? I don't remember having a choice either. You made that choice for both of us."

He stared at her in disbelief. "You're a piece of work, Kelly. Still the innocent martyr, I see."

She walked over to the door and opened it, looking expectantly at him.

He didn't move. "Why are you living this way, Kelly? I can't wrap my head around why you did what you did. I would have given you everything. Hell, I still gave you a hefty amount of money when we broke up because I didn't like to think of you being without. But now I find you living in squalor working a job that is far beneath your abilities."

A wave of hatred hit her hard. In this moment she realized that she truly loved and hated him in equal measure. Her chest hurt so bad that she couldn't breathe. Her mind went back to the day when she'd stood in front of him, devastated, completely and utterly broken, while he scribbled his signature on a bank draft and disdainfully shoved it toward her.

The look in his eyes had told her that he didn't love her, had never loved her. He didn't trust her. He didn't have faith in her.

When she'd needed him the absolute most, he'd let her down and treated her like a paid whore.

She would *never* forgive him for that.

She slowly turned and dragged herself over to the kitchen drawer where she kept the crumpled envelope containing the check. A reminder of broken dreams and ultimate betrayal. She'd looked at it often but had sworn she would never walk into a bank and cash it.

She picked it up and walked back over to where he stood, his expression inscrutable. She crumpled the envelope into a ball and hurled it at him, hitting him in the cheek.

"There's your check," she hissed. "Take it and get the hell out of my life."

He bent slowly and retrieved the balled-up envelope. He unfolded it and then opened it, taking out the worn check. He frowned and then stared back at her. “I don’t understand.”

“You’ve never understood,” she whispered. “Since you won’t leave, I’m out of here.”

Before he could stop her, she walked past him and slammed the door behind her.

Ryan stared at the check in his hand in stunned disbelief, unable to formulate his thoughts. Why? She acted as though he was a piece of scum. What the hell had he ever done to her but make sure she was taken care of?

He glanced around at the efficiency apartment, noting the disrepair and the cheapness of the furnishings. Two cabinet doors were barely hanging on their hinges and there was nothing inside. No food.

With a frown he stalked to the refrigerator and threw open the door. He cursed when he saw only a carton of milk, half a package of cheese and a jar of peanut butter.

He hastily rummaged through the rest of the kitchen, growing more furious when he found nothing more. How was she surviving? Furthermore, why was she living like this?

He glanced back down at the check and shook his head. There were enough zeros in the amount for her to live a good, modest life for years to come.

The ink had run in several places and it was smudged with fingerprints. But she'd never tried to cash it. Why? There were so many questions running around in his head that he couldn't process them all.

Did she feel guilty over what she'd done? Had she been ashamed to take money from him after betraying him?

Not the best time to develop a conscience.

One thing was for certain. He wasn't leaving. There were too many unanswered questions and he wanted answers. Why was she here in this run-down place with a job that obviously didn't net her enough money to feed herself, much less live a comfortable life? What in the world was she going to do when the baby came? Whether it was his baby or not, he couldn't allow himself to walk away. Not when she had meant so much to him.

She wasn't taking care of herself. He had

always taken care of her in the past and he would do it again. Whether she liked it or not.

Kelly cut behind her apartment complex using the side street. She didn't go back to work, although it was what she should do. A day's lost wages wasn't the end of the world, but the tips she missed would be a blow to her meager savings.

She needed time to think. To compose herself. And Ryan would only go back to the diner to force another confrontation.

The rain had stopped but the skies were still cast in gloomy shades of gray with more black clouds in the distance, a sure signal that the rain wasn't over for the day.

Tears threatened, much like those ominous storm clouds, but she sucked in her breath—determined not to allow her unexpected face-to-face with Ryan to break her.

The small playground just three blocks from her apartment was abandoned. No children playing. The swings were empty, swaying in the breeze and the merry-go-round creaked as it rotated slowly.

She slid onto one of the benches, her mind in chaos from the bombardment of anger, grief and shock.

Why had he come?

Her pregnancy was obviously a huge surprise to him. There was no faking the what-the-hell expression on his face in the diner. Nor was their meeting some bizarre coincidence.

She'd given their relationship a lot of thought over the past months, when she wasn't doing everything possible to make herself forget him. Like that was going to happen.

She knew several things. One, they'd moved way too fast. From their meeting in the café where she'd served him coffee to their rush engagement, she hadn't taken the time to be sure of him. Oh, she'd been plenty sure of herself. She'd fallen head over heels from the first look. She'd allowed herself to be swept into a relationship with him, never questioning his commitment to her. Or his love.

The obstacles then had seemed insignificant.

He was out of her league, but she'd naively assumed that love would conquer all and that it didn't matter if his family or friends disapproved. She would prove herself worthy. She'd fit in with his lifestyle.

No, she didn't have his money, his connections, his breeding or heritage. But who even cared about that stuff in this day and age?

She'd been stupid. She'd put off school, at least temporarily, because she'd been consumed with being the perfect girlfriend, fiancée and eventually wife to Ryan Beardsley. She'd allowed him to outfit her in the finest clothing. She'd moved into his apartment with him. She'd agonized over saying the right thing and being the ideal complement to his life.

And she'd never had a chance.

Anyone who thought love was a cure for all things was a misguided fool. Maybe if he'd loved her enough—or at all. How could he ever have loved her when he turned on her at the first opportunity?

She closed her eyes against the unwanted sting of tears. She'd fled New York and ended up here in Houston. She'd forged a new life for herself. It wasn't the best life, but it was hers.

She'd known that she couldn't go back to school until after her baby was born and so she'd worked and saved every penny for that eventuality. She lived in the cheapest apartment she could find and earmarked all her earnings for when her child arrived. Then she would move into a better place, somewhere safe to raise a child and complete the two semesters she had left of school so she could make a better life for both herself and her precious baby. Without Ryan Beardsley and his filthy money and his horrid family and all the mistrust and betrayal she'd been subjected to.

Now… Now what? Why was Ryan here? And what would his discovery of her pregnancy mean for her future? Her plans? Her determination never to allow herself back into a situation where she risked so much hurt and devastation?

She rubbed her forehead tiredly, willing the ache to go away. She was tired, worn thin and in no position to defend herself from whatever onslaught Ryan was preparing.

Her fingers tightened and anger penetrated the haze. Why the hell was she sitting on a park bench hiding? She wasn't in the wrong. Ryan couldn't make her do anything he wanted; and, furthermore, he would leave her apartment or she'd get a restraining order against him.

He had no power over her anymore.

She breathed in deeply, steadying her shot nerves. Yeah, he'd caught her off guard. She hadn't been prepared to see him again. But that didn't mean she was going to let him mow over her.

Even as she made that resolution, nervous fear fluttered in her chest and tightened her throat. The future that she'd planned suddenly seemed in peril with Ryan's reappearance in her life.

If he got it in his head that it was his child she carried, he wouldn't go away. The problem was, even if she managed to convince him that it wasn't his child, he'd only assume it was Jarrod's. That still made the Beardsley family a serious impediment to her future.

"One thing at a time, Kelly," she murmured.

The very first thing she had to do was get

Ryan out of her apartment so she could weigh her options. She may not have his money or connections but that didn't mean she was going to fold at the first sign of adversity.

A raindrop hit her forehead and she sighed. It had begun sprinkling again, and if she didn't get back, she'd be caught out in the downpour that was surely coming.

As she trudged in the direction of her building she cheered herself up by imagining that he wouldn't be there. That he'd given up and left, deciding she wasn't worth the effort. She snorted as that thought crossed her mind. He'd already done that once. It wasn't a stretch that he'd simply dismiss her from his life again.

By the time she climbed the stairs to her apartment, she was soaked through and her hair clung limply to her head. She shivered as she fumbled with the lock to let herself in.

It didn't surprise her to see Ryan pacing the floor of her living room. She stiffened her shoulders just as he whirled around.

"Where the hell have you been?" he demanded.

"None of your business."

"The hell it's not. You didn't go back to work. It's raining and you're soaked to the skin. Are you crazy?"

She laughed and shook her head. "Clearly I am. Or I was. But not anymore. Get out, Ryan. This is my apartment. You have no rights here. You can't bully your way in here. I'll swear out a restraining order if I have to."

His forehead wrinkled and he stared at her in surprise. "You think I'd hurt you?"

She lifted a shoulder in a shrug. "Physically? No."

He swore under his breath. Then he ran his hand through his hair in agitation. "You need to eat. There's no food in this apartment. How the hell are you taking care of yourself and a baby when you're on your feet all day? You're clearly not eating here. There's nothing to eat!"

"My, my, one would think you cared," she mocked. "But we both know that isn't true. Don't worry about me, Ryan. I'm taking care of myself and my baby just fine."

He stalked toward her, his eyes blazing. "Oh, I care, Kelly. You can't accuse me of not caring.

I wasn't the one who threw away what we had. That's on you. Not me."

She held up a hand and hastily backed away. Her fingers trembled and she felt precariously light-headed. "Get. Out."

His nostrils flared and his lip curled up as if he was about to launch another offensive. Then he took a step back and blew out his breath.

"I'll leave, but I'll be back at nine tomorrow morning."

She lifted one eyebrow.

"You have an appointment to see a doctor. I'm taking you."

He'd been busy while she was gone, and he worked fast. But then for a man like Ryan, all he had to do was pick up a phone. He had countless people to do his bidding. She shook her head in disgust. "Maybe you don't get it, Ryan. I'm not going anywhere with you. We are nothing to each other. You aren't responsible for me. I have my own doctor. You aren't hauling me to another one."

"And when was the last time you saw this doctor?" he demanded. "You look like hell,

Kelly. You aren't taking care of yourself. That can't be good for either you or your child."

"Don't pretend that you care," she said softly. "Just do us both a favor and leave."

He looked like he was going to argue, but again, he bit back the words. He walked toward the door and then turned around to her again. "Nine o'clock tomorrow. You're going if I have to carry you there myself."

"Yeah, and maybe hell will freeze over," she muttered as he slammed out of her apartment.

She woke up early as a matter of habit. A quick check of her watch, however, told her she had overslept by fifteen minutes. She would have to hurry to get to the diner by six. After a brief shower, she pulled on her loose-fitting jumper over a shirt and headed for the door.

She held her breath, almost expecting Ryan to be outside. She shook her head and walked down the stairs. He was messing with her head and making her paranoid. Any thought that she was over him and moving on had been shot to hell the moment he showed up in her diner.

A few minutes later, she hustled into the diner to see that Nina was already at work serving their early-morning breakfast customers. Kelly donned her apron, picked up her order tablet and headed toward her section of tables.

For the first hour, she forced thoughts of Ryan and the dread that he'd make another appearance to the back of her mind. Unfortunately, it was obvious that she failed miserably after she messed up three orders, spilled coffee on a customer and retreated to the kitchen to get herself together.

She'd just given herself a stern lecture, calmed her shaking hands and was preparing to return out front when Ralph burst through the doors, a scowl on his face.

"What the hell are you doing here?"

Kelly frowned. "I work here, remember?"

"Not anymore you don't. You're out of here."

Kelly paled and stared at him as panic rolled through her chest. "You're firing me?"

"You walked out yesterday during our busiest time. No word, no nothing. You didn't come back. What the hell did you expect? And now you're back here this morning and I have a diner full of pissed-off customers because you don't have your head on right."

She took a deep breath and tried to steady her nerves. "Ralph, I need this job. Yesterday… Yesterday I got sick, okay? It won't happen again."

"Damn right it won't. I never should have hired you in the first place." He curled his lip in disgust. "If I hadn't needed a waitress so desperately, I would have never hired a pregnant woman to begin with."

Oh God, she didn't want to beg, but what choice did she have? The chances of her finding another job at this advanced stage of pregnancy were nil. All she needed was a few more months, just until the baby was born. By then she'd have enough money to stop working and take care of her baby. She'd have enough money to finish the rest of her classes.

"Please," she choked out. "Give me another chance. You've never heard a single complaint from me. I've never missed work for any reason. I have to have this job."

He pulled out an envelope from his shirt

pocket and thrust it toward her. "Here's your final check, minus the hours for yesterday's disappearing act."

She took it with a shaking hand and he turned and walked out of the kitchen, the door swinging wildly behind him.

Anger and frustration overwhelmed her. Ryan was still ruining her life, months later. She yanked off her apron, tossed it in the direction of the hook and then left through the back entrance, squinting when she was nearly blinded by sunlight.

As she walked back toward her apartment, she stared at the envelope in her hand. Despair weighed her down until each step felt unbearable. Her damn pride. She should have taken the check Ryan had given her. To hell with him and his nasty accusations. That check represented a way for her to finish school and provide for her child.

She had every reason to refuse it. To tear it up into little pieces and shove it under his nose. Maybe that's why she'd held on to it for so long because a part of her wanted the satisfaction of throwing it back at him.

It had been important to her that he know she wasn't some whore to be bought, but what had that got her? A dead-end job that sucked the life out of her on a daily basis and a shabby apartment that she never wanted to bring her child home to.

Enough with her pride. Ryan Beardsley could go to hell. She was going to cash that check.

Three

Ryan mounted the steps to Kelly's apartment, grimacing as he took in the missing handrail and the shaky stairs. It was a wonder she hadn't already fallen down them. He wasn't entirely expecting to find her home, but he'd stopped in at the diner in case she'd gone to work, only to be told by a surly man named Ralph that she wasn't there.

It annoyed him that her door wasn't locked. He pushed it open to find her on her hands and knees, peering under the rickety recliner. She made a sound of frustration and then pushed herself upward.

"What the hell are you doing?"

She shrieked and whirled around. "Get out!"

He held out a placating hand. "I'm sorry I frightened you. Your door was unlocked."

"And so you thought you'd just come on in? Did the art of knocking escape you? Get a clue, Ryan. I don't want you here." She went into the kitchen, opening and shutting cabinets, obviously looking for something.

He sighed. It wasn't that he'd expected her to be any more compliant today, but he'd hoped after the initial shock, she'd be a little less… angry.

When she got back down on the floor again, a surge of irritation hit him once more.

He crossed the room and leaned down to help her to her feet. "What are you looking for?"

She shrugged off his hand and wiped her hair from her eyes. "The check. I'm looking for the check!"

"What check?"

"The check you wrote me."

He frowned and reached into his pocket for the folded, worn piece of paper. "This check?"

She lunged for it but he held it higher out of her reach.

"Yes! I've changed my mind. I'm cashing it."

He put his hand out to ward her off and shook his head in confusion. "Sit down, Kelly, before you fall. And then tell me what on earth is going on here. You wait this long, throw the check in my face and tell me to take my money to hell with me and now you've changed your mind? Are you crazy?"

To his utter surprise, she slumped down onto one of the small chairs that accompanied the two person table in the kitchen and buried her face in her hands. To his further dismay, her shoulders shook and quiet sobs erupted from her bowed head.

For a moment he stood there, unsure what to do. He'd never been able to stand it when she cried. An uncomfortable feeling settled in his stomach and he dropped down to one knee to gently pry her hands from her face.

She looked away, seemingly discomfited by the fact he was witnessing her breakdown.

"What's wrong, Kelly?" he asked gently.

"I lost my job," she choked out. "Because of you."

He reared back. "Because of me? What the hell did I do?"

She whipped her head up, her eyes flashing. "Your standard line. What did I do? Of course you did nothing wrong. I'm sure this was all my fault, like everything else that went wrong in our relationship. Just give me the check and get out. You won't ever have to be bothered with me again."

He stared incredulously at her. "Do you honestly expect me to just walk away *now?*" He shoved the check back into his pocket, his lips thin as he controlled the urge to lash out at her as she had done to him. "We have a hell of a lot to work out, Kelly. I'm not going anywhere and neither are you. The very first thing we're going to do is go to the doctor so you can get a decent checkup. You don't look well. I can't be any more blunt than that."

She slowly stood and stared him in the eye. "I'm not going anywhere with you. If you won't give me the check, then get out. We have nothing more to discuss. Ever."

He fingered the paper in his pocket and then lifted his gaze to meet hers once more. "We'll discuss the check after we go to the doctor."

Disgust flared in her eyes. "Resorting to blackmail now, Ryan?"

"If that's what you want to call it. I really don't care. You're going to the doctor with me. If he gives you a clean bill of health, then I'll hand over the check and walk out of here."

Her eyes narrowed suspiciously. "Just like that."

He nodded, not bothering to tell her that there wasn't a doctor in this world who could possibly give her a clean bill of health. She was dead on her feet. She was pale and very likely significantly underweight.

She nibbled at her lip for a long while as if deciding whether or not to acquiesce. Then finally she closed her eyes and let out her breath in a long exhale.

"All right, Ryan. I'll go to the doctor with you.

After he verifies that I'm perfectly fine, I don't want to see you again."

"*If* he says you're okay, then you'll get your wish."

She lowered herself back into the chair, clearly exhausted. He bit back a curse. Was she blind or just that heavily into denial? She needed someone to take care of her. Make sure she ate three good meals a day. Someone to make her put her feet up and rest.

He checked his watch. "We should be going. Your appointment is in half an hour and I don't know how bad traffic will be."

Defeat crept over her face, but then she hardened her expression and rose once more. She retrieved her purse from the recliner and started for the door, leaving him to follow.

Kelly stared sightlessly out the window as Ryan maneuvered through traffic. She was mentally exhausted from her confrontation with Ryan. She just wanted him gone. She couldn't even look at him without all the hurt from the past crashing through her and turning her inside out.

He parked in the garage of a downtown medical clinic and ushered her inside the modern building. They rode the elevator to the fourth floor and Kelly stood numbly as Ryan checked in with the receptionist.

After filling out her medical history, she was ushered back for the prerequisite pee in a cup. When she exited the bathroom, a nurse directed her into one of the exam rooms where she found Ryan waiting for her.

She bared her teeth in a snarl, prepared to order him out when he held up a hand, his expression as fierce as her own had to be.

"I will hear firsthand everything the doctor has to say."

His eyes dared her to argue. She swallowed nervously, knowing he'd make a scene if she pushed the issue. She turned her back on him and leaned on the exam table.

She just had to get past the exam, have the doctor tell Ryan that everything was fine, and then she'd be rid of him.

A few minutes later, a young doctor came in and smiled at her. He gestured for her to get onto the table and recline. After measuring her and listening to the baby's heartbeat, he wheeled in a small machine and then applied cool gel to her stomach.

She lifted her head. "What are you doing?"

"Thought you might like to get a look at the little guy or girl. I'll do a quick sonogram for dates and measurement, make sure everything is okay. Is that all right with you?"

She nodded and the doctor began moving the wand over her stomach. Then he stopped and gestured toward the small screen. "There's the head."

Ryan crowded in so he could see the monitor. She craned her neck to see around him. Ryan looked back at her then hastily slipped a hand underneath her neck to lift her so she could see. Tears filled her eyes and her lips widened into a smile. "She's beautiful!"

"Yes, she is," Ryan said huskily in her ear.

"Or he," she said quickly.

"Would you like to find out what you're having?" the doctor offered. "We can take a look."

"No...no, I don't think so," she said. "I want it to be a surprise."

The doctor took a few more minutes and then stood up, wiping her belly clean. He handed her a picture he printed out of the baby's profile and returned to his clipboard. After a few scribbled notes, he looked back up at her. "I'm concerned about you."

She frowned and struggled to sit up. Ryan eased her into a sitting position, and she looked questioningly at the doctor.

"Your blood pressure is elevated and there are traces of protein in your urine. There is significant edema to your hands and feet and I'd bet, judging by your weight, that you aren't getting enough nutrition. You're exhibiting signs of preeclampsia and it could lead to serious repercussions."

Kelly regarded him in stunned silence.

Ryan turned to the doctor with a frown. "What is preeclampsia?"

"It's related to an increase in blood pressure and an increase in protein in urine output. Typically it affects women after their twentieth week of pregnancy. It can progress to seizures, at that point it becomes eclampsia."

The doctor turned his stern gaze on Kelly before continuing.

"You are only a hairbreadth from going into the hospital and staying there until you deliver, and unless I exact a promise from you and your husband that you'll remain off your feet and take better care of yourself, I'll forgo the warning and straight into the hospital you'll go."

"He's not my—" she began.

"Consider it done," Ryan smoothly interjected. "She won't so much as lift a finger. You have my word."

"But—"

"No buts," the doctor said. "I don't think you fully understand the direness of your situation. If your condition progresses, it can mean your death. Eclampsia is the second leading cause of maternal death in the U.S. and the leading cause of fetal complications. This is serious and you need to take all the necessary precautions to prevent an escalation in your condition."

Ryan blanched, and she felt the blood drain from her own face as well.

"I can assure you, Doctor, Kelly won't be doing anything but resting and eating from now on," Ryan said grimly.

The doctor nodded approvingly and shook both their hands. "I'd like to see her back in a week. And if the swelling gets worse or she develops a severe headache she's to go directly to the hospital."

After the doctor left, Kelly sat on the exam table, stunned by the doctor's pronouncement. Ryan slid his hand over hers and squeezed.

"I don't want you to worry, Kelly."

Worry? She nearly let out a hysterical laugh. Her life was a total and complete mess and she wasn't supposed to worry. She was ready to run screaming from the building.

"Come on," he said quietly. "Let's go."

She let him lead her out of the doctor's office and to the car without protest. This couldn't be happening to her. She sat mutely in the car as they drove away, refusing to even look at Ryan. She had no job, and now if the doctor was to be believed, she couldn't have worked even if she hadn't been fired. How was she going to support herself, let alone her baby? She had some savings but it was all earmarked for the baby and school.

Helplessness gripped her and she didn't like it one bit. The shrill ring of a cell phone startled her and she looked over to see Ryan put it to his ear as he expertly weaved through traffic. Her ears perked up when she heard her name.

"We're going by Kelly's apartment to get her things. Book us a flight from Houston and call me back with the flight number and time. Then call over to Dr. Whitcomb's office on Hillcrest and get Kelly's medical report faxed to Dr. Bryant in New York. Cover for me and have Linda go over any contracts needing my signatures. I'll be in the office in a few days."

He ended the conversation abruptly and set the phone aside.

"What were you talking about?" Kelly said in bewilderment.

He glanced over at her, a grim expression tightening his face. "I'm taking you home."

"Over my dead body," she snarled. She crossed her arms over her belly and pressed her lips firmly together.

"You're going," he said in a tone that brooked no argument. "You need someone to take care of you since you refuse to do it yourself. Do you want to risk the baby's health? Or yours? Give me a solution, Kelly. Prove to me that I can leave here knowing you'll be okay."

She stared woodenly at him. "Don't you understand that I want nothing to do with you?"

"Oh yes, you made that clear to me when you slept with my brother. But the fact is you're likely carrying my child—or my niece or nephew, and either way I'm not going to disappear until I know you're both safe. You're coming to New York with me if I have to carry you on the plane."

"It's not your child," she said fiercely.

His gaze raked over her. "Whose is it then?"

"None of your business."

There was a long silence before he finally said, "You're going with me. I'm not just doing this for a child that may or may not be mine."

"Why are you doing it then?" she shot back.

He ignored her and stared out the windshield, his fingers curled tight around the steering wheel.

When they arrived at her apartment, she got out of the car before he could come around for her and she hurried up the stairs. She could hear him behind her and when she tried to shut the door, he put up his hand and pushed his way inside.

"We have to talk, Kelly."

She whirled around. "Yes, we do. You said we'd talk about the check. You were certainly willing to throw it at me when you called me a whore. I want it now and I don't give a damn what you think about the fact I'm taking it."

"I'm no longer offering it."

"Oh, nice," she said sarcastically.

"I want you to come back to New York with me."

Her mouth fell open. "You're insane. Why would I go anywhere with you?"

"Because you need me."

Pain speared through her chest, robbing her of breath. "I needed you before."

She turned away before he could respond. She framed her belly with her palms and tried not to panic.

Behind her Ryan was silent. Disturbingly so. Then when he spoke there was an odd, strained tone to his voice.

"I'm going out to have your prescriptions filled. I'll pick us up something to eat. When I get back, I want you to be packed."

His footsteps were heavy on the floor and then the door shut quietly behind him.

She sank onto the tattered recliner and massaged her forehead. Two days ago she had a plan. A good plan. She had everything mapped out. Today she had no job, her health was suspect and her ex-fiancé was pressuring her to go back to New York with him.

It made her cringe, but she realized she was going to have to call her mother. She'd once sworn she'd have to be dying to ever ask her mom for anything, but right now that seemed the lesser of two evils.

"What doesn't kill me will make me stronger, right?" she muttered.

Lame. So lame.

Still, she picked up the phone, drew in a deep breath and called the last number she had for her mother. It was entirely possible Deidre no longer lived in Florida. Who really knew with her?

She'd washed her hands of Kelly the minute Kelly graduated high school and all but shoved her out of the house so she could move in her latest boyfriend. She'd informed Kelly that she'd done her duty and devoted eighteen of the best years of her life—years she'd never get back—to raising a child she'd never intended to have.

Good luck, see you later, don't ask me for anything else.

Yeah.

Kelly was about to hang up when her mother's voice came over the line.

"Mom?" Kelly said hesitantly.

There was a long pause. "Kelly? Is that you?"

"Yeah, Mom it's me. Look, I need your help. I need a place to stay. I'm…pregnant."

There was an even longer pause this time. "Where's that rich boyfriend of yours?"

"I'm not with him any longer," Kelly said in a

quiet voice. "I'm in Houston. I lost my job and I'm not well. The doctor is worried about the baby. I just need a place to stay for a little while. Until I get back on my feet."

Her mother sighed. "I can't help you, Kelly. Richard and I are busy and we just don't have the space."

Hurt crowded into her heart. She'd known this was pointless, but somehow she'd hoped... Quietly, she turned the phone off without saying anything else. What was there to say anyway?

Her mother had never been more than a resigned babysitter.

Kelly smoothed a hand over her belly. "I love you," she whispered. "I'll never begrudge a single moment I have with you."

She leaned back in the recliner and stared up at the ceiling, hating the helplessness that gripped her. She closed her eyes in weary resignation. She was exhausted.

The next thing she knew she was being shaken awake. She yanked her eyes open to see Ryan standing over her, a plate and glass of water in his hands.

"I brought you Thai," he said gruffly.

Her favorite. She was surprised he remembered. She struggled to sit upright and then took the plate and glass from him.

He pulled a chair from the kitchen and sat across from her as she ate. His scrutiny made her uncomfortable and so she focused on her food, not looking up.

"Ignoring me isn't going to help."

She paused, set her fork down and then leveled a stare at him. "What do you want, Ryan? I still don't understand why you're here. Or why you want me to go back to New York with you. Or why you care, period. You let me know in no uncertain terms that you wanted me as far out of your life as possible."

"You're pregnant. You need help. Isn't that enough?"

"No, it's not!"

His jaw tightened. "Let's put it this way. You and I have a lot to work out, including whether or not you're pregnant with my child. You need help that I can provide. You need someone to take care of you. You need top-notch medical care. I can give you all of those things."

She thrust a hand into her hair and leaned back against the recliner. He immediately leaned forward, slipping from his chair and going to his knees in front of her. He touched her arm, tentatively, as if afraid she'd recoil.

"Come with me, Kelly. You know this has to be worked out between us. You have to think about the baby."

She held up a hand, furious that he'd try to manipulate her with guilt. But he caught her hand and lowered it, and then ruthlessly pressed his advantage.

"You can't work. The doctor said you have to rest or you risk the health of your child as well as your own. If you can't accept my help for yourself, at least do it for your baby. Or is your pride more important than his or her welfare?"

"And what are we supposed to do when we get to New York, Ryan?"

"You're going to rest and we're going to figure out our future."

Her stomach lurched. It sounded so ominous. Their future.

She was a fool to agree. She'd be a fool not to agree.

She was willing to swallow her pride and take the check. Shouldn't she be willing to accept his help for her baby's sake? For their baby's sake?

"Kelly?"

"I'll go," she said in a low voice.

Triumph flashed in his eyes. "Then let's get you packed and get the hell out of here."

Four

When Kelly woke the next morning, she struggled to make sense of her surroundings. Then she remembered. She was in New York—with Ryan.

In a matter of hours, Ryan had had her packed and hustled to the airport. They'd landed at LaGuardia close to midnight and he'd ushered her into a waiting car.

By the time they'd arrived at his apartment, she was dead on her feet. Once inside, she took her one bag and headed toward the guest room. The aching familiarity of the apartment—an apartment that used to be hers—threatened to unhinge her. It even smelled the same—a mixture of leather and raw masculinity. She'd never tried to change that. It had reminded her too much of Ryan, and she hadn't wanted to remove it.

Down the hall was the bedroom where she and Ryan had made love countless times. It was where their child was conceived and where her life had been irrevocably altered.

Once again, she'd been reminded of how much of an idiot she was to come back here.

But this morning she felt resigned to her fate. After a quick shower, she dressed and padded into the living room where Ryan was already sitting typing on a laptop. He looked up when he heard her come in.

"Breakfast is ready. I was waiting on you to eat."

Wordlessly, she followed him into the kitchen where she saw a table set for two. Taking a platter off the warmer, he carried it over to the table and began spooning healthy portions of eggs, toast and ham onto their plates.

As she sat down, she was forced to admit that

she felt better than she had in weeks. She had certainly gotten more rest in the past twenty-four hours than she had in a long time.

"How are you feeling this morning?" he asked as he took a seat across from her.

"Fine," she mumbled around a mouthful of egg. Her appetite was coming back and she concentrated on the delicious food in front of her.

This whole thing was weird. The ultrapoliteness. The cozy breakfast for two. It was so awkward that she wanted to go back to the bedroom and crawl back into bed.

After a long silence, Ryan spoke up. "I've made arrangements to work out of the apartment for the time being."

She stopped chewing then swallowed the food in her mouth. "Why?" she asked flatly.

"I would think the answer is obvious."

"This isn't going to work, Ryan. I can't stay here with you hanging over my shoulder all the time. Go to work. Do whatever it is you normally do, and just leave me alone."

His lips thinned and then he got up and walked away without another word.

She stared down at her plate, furious that he acted like the victim. As if she was some horrible, ungrateful bitch.

Fury and aching sadness knotted her throat. How could she ever get past what he'd done to her? Maybe he was just as determined not to forgive her for her supposed transgressions, but Kelly was the innocent one in this whole sordid mess. Ryan had turned his back on her. He didn't seem to want to acknowledge that little fact.

She fiddled with her remaining food, pushing it around her plate until restlessness forced her to her feet.

Wandering aimlessly back into the living room, she stopped in front of the large window offering a view of the Manhattan skyline.

"You shouldn't be on your feet," Ryan said from behind her.

She sighed and turned around, shocked to see him in just a towel. She swiveled back to the window, but the image burned in her eyes. His broad chest rippled with well-defined muscles and his lean abdomen was sculpted like a fine work of art. She used to spend hours exploring the dips and curves of his body.

"I'm sorry if I embarrassed you," he said in a low voice. "I guess I didn't give it a thought considering our past relationship."

She had the ridiculous urge to laugh. Embarrass her? The only embarrassing thing was how her mind was currently wandering way below the makeshift waistline of his towel.

And of course, in his arrogance, he would assume—considering the "nature of their relationship"—that he could cavort about in the nude.

Drawing up her shoulders, she turned around again and stared coolly at him. "If you think because we were once lovers that you can take up where we left off, you're sadly mistaken."

He blinked in surprise and then anger replaced the surprise. "God, Kelly. Do you think so little of me that I would try to force you into a sexual relationship when you're pregnant and unwell?"

"You don't want to know the answer to that."

He swore long and hard. "What makes you

think I would ever want to sample my brother's secondhand goods anyway?"

She balled her hands into fists and forced a careless reply. "Well, since your brother didn't mind, I assumed it was a family trait."

His blue eyes became ice chips and his jaw twitched spasmodically. Then he spun around and disappeared into his bedroom, the sound of the door slamming reverberating throughout the apartment.

Kelly sighed and sank into a nearby armchair. What demon had forced her to throw more fuel on the flames she would never know. The need to defend herself had long since fled. He should have believed in her *then.* She didn't really care what he chose to do now. The desire for him to stand behind her and protect her had fizzled when she realized that she'd *never* had his love or his faith.

God, what was she doing here? Just being in New York again brought back too many memories she would be better off forgetting.

Restless and sick at heart, she made her way back into the kitchen and took stock of the contents of the refrigerator and cabinets. Deciding that she had all the necessary ingredients for one of her favorite dishes, she began laying them out on the countertop. At least it would give her something to do and lunch would be taken care of. She'd always loved to cook for Ryan when they lived together.

"What the hell do you think you're doing?" Ryan demanded, materializing out of nowhere and taking the pan she was holding from her. He steered her firmly away from the counter and back into the living room. "Sit," he ordered once they reached the couch. He propped her feet up on the coffee table, placing a pillow under them. He stood back, his expression lacking the anger of just a few minutes ago.

"Maybe you didn't understand the doctor's orders. You're to rest. Stay off your feet." He enunciated each word in clipped tones as if he were speaking to a dolt. Well, that wasn't entirely untrue. She was the biggest dolt in the world for getting caught up in this mess.

He seemed calm. And she was calm, too—at

least for now. It was time to get things out in the open. "Ryan, we need to talk."

He looked surprised and a little wary over her change in tone, but he sat down across from her and regarded her with open curiosity. "Okay, talk."

"I want to know why you came to Houston." She was careful to keep her emotions in check as she waited for his response.

He didn't look pleased with her question. He looked away, at the wall, his jaw tight.

"And how did you know where to find me?" she continued when he remained silent.

"I hired an investigator," he said after a moment's pause.

Her mouth fell open. So much for being calm. "Why? So you could accuse me of being a whore all over again? So you could sweep in and upend my life? I don't get it, Ryan. You hate me. I know what you think of me. You made it very clear when you threw me out of your life. Why the hell would you come looking to dig up the past again?"

"Damn it, Kelly!" he exploded. "You disappeared without a word to anyone. You didn't cash the check. I thought you were out there hurt and scared—or dead."

"Too bad for you I wasn't."

"Don't you make this about me," he growled. It was obvious he had only a tenuous grip on his control. "You took what we had and threw it in my face. *You* decided I wasn't enough for you. I looked for you because no matter what you had done or how badly I wanted to forget you, I couldn't stand the thought of you being out there somewhere scared and alone."

He broke off and looked away. When he looked back at her, his eyes were shuttered. "I've answered your questions, now I want mine answered."

They both glanced up at the sound of the front door opening and, to Kelly's horror, Ryan's brother, Jarrod, stood in the entryway. "Hey Ryan, the doorman told me you were back…." His voice died when he saw her. "Uh…hi, Kelly."

Ryan watched as Kelly's expression became glacial. Damn it, she was going to think he planned this. And while yes, the three of them certainly needed to hash out a few things, now wasn't the time. He rose from his seat and headed in his brother's direction.

It had taken Ryan months to see beyond his rage and jealousy to be able to entertain resuming a normal relationship with his younger brother. Before Ryan hadn't given a second thought to Jarrod coming and going at will. He had a key. Ryan had always encouraged him to drop in and had looked forward to his visits.

But that was before Jarrod had slept with Kelly. Before the two most important people in his life had betrayed him. When he finally talked himself around to forgiving Jarrod and allowing him back into his life, he'd also considered that if he was willing to forgive his brother then perhaps he should also find Kelly and at least listen to her reasons why.

Things weren't perfect between him and his brother now. Maybe they never would be. But they were better and Jarrod had started coming around more, even if he was more cautious than he'd ever been in the past.

Now Ryan had brought Kelly back and they'd

all be forced to face the inevitable confrontation. A part of him dreaded it, but the other part of him knew he'd never be able to move forward unless this was fully resolved. But it would be done when he decided and not before. He and Kelly had too much to work out between them before they tackled the issue of Jarrod and her infidelity.

"This isn't a good time, man," he said in a low voice when he reached his brother.

Unease flickered across Jarrod's face, and he glanced nervously over Ryan's shoulder toward Kelly. "I can see that. I'll come back another time."

Ryan turned and saw Kelly tremble and then her fingers flexed and curled into fists. She was as pale as death, her eyes large and haunted."What did you want?" he prompted when Jarrod made no move to leave.

"Nothing important. Just came over to say hi and to tell you Mom wanted us over for dinner Saturday night. I hadn't seen you in a while. I know you've been busy with your resort deal. I'd hoped we could get together like old times."

Ryan sighed. He and Jarrod had always been close. Until Kelly. He hated this. Hated it all. Hated that a woman had come between him and the brother he'd all but raised after their father died.

"I'll call Mom later, okay? And we'll get together. Just not right now."

"Yeah, I understand. I'll see you later." He backed toward the door, and Ryan followed. As Ryan gripped the doorknob to close it after Jarrod, his brother whispered, "Are you taking her back after what happened?"

Ryan drew his brows together. "Aren't you concerned that she could be carrying your child?"

Jarrod flinched and his cheeks lost color. "Is that what she told you?"

Ryan studied him for a moment, his brows drawing together as he observed Jarrod's reaction to the suggestion. "No, she didn't tell me that, but surely you know it's possible."

"Uh-uh, can't be mine," Jarrod said, shaking his head emphatically.

"So you say."

Jarrod stepped into the hall and then shoved

his hands into his pockets as he stared back at Ryan. But he didn't quite meet Ryan's gaze. "I wore protection. Look, I'm sorry. I know this is a bad situation. But the baby can't be mine."

Ryan watched him walk toward the elevator, the same frustrated helplessness clutching his throat. He stepped back and shut the door, angry. Angry at Kelly, angry at Jarrod and angry with himself all over again. So the baby was his unless…surely she hadn't had other partners besides him and Jarrod. He wouldn't even give that consideration.

When he returned to the couch he wasn't prepared for the absolute hatred and revulsion in Kelly's expression. Before he could say anything she fixed him with a look that froze him to the bone.

"If he ever comes over here again, I'm out of here. I won't be in the same room with him."

Ryan was taken aback. "You know he's here all the time."

Her teeth were clenched and her knuckles white. "I won't stay here."

Why the hell was she so angry with Jarrod? If

anyone deserved to be angry it was Jarrod, after Kelly had accused him of trying to rape her. Nothing about this entire situation made sense. And he was tired of trying to figure it out.

"Jarrod said he wore protection," he said, gauging her reaction.

Pain rippled across her face. Not the reaction he'd imagined. "And of course you believed him," she said in a voice that sounded like she was dangerously close to tears.

"Are you saying he didn't? Are you maintaining the baby is mine?" He'd had no idea how badly he wanted the baby to be his until now. His eyes pleaded with her to confirm it. To say that *he* was the father.

The indecipherable mask was back on her face again. "I don't maintain anything," she said, frost dripping from her voice.

Frustration hit him like a ton of bricks. She had shut herself off again and nothing was going to open her to him. He wanted to put his fist through the wall.

"I'm going out for a while," he finally ground out. "I'll bring back lunch."

He turned and stalked out before he said things he'd only regret.

As he made his way to the underground garage where his BMW was parked, his cell phone rang, rudely intruding on his thoughts. "What?" he barked into the receiver.

"Ryan?" His mom's voice bled through his dour mood.

"Sorry, Mom, didn't mean to snap." He opened the door and slid into the seat, settling back, not bothering to start the engine yet.

"Ryan, what's wrong?"

"Nothing, Mom, just a busy day. What's up?"

"I was hoping you and Jarrod would have dinner with me tomorrow night."

Ryan closed his eyes, pinching the bridge of his nose between two fingers. There was no easy way to say this and his mom would know soon enough now that Jarrod had been over. Best she know now so she could get used to it. "Mom, you should know…Kelly is with me…and she's pregnant."

There was a sharp intake of breath on the other end followed by thick silence. "I see," she finally said. "I guess inviting Roberta is out of the question."

Ryan blew out his breath at his mother's snippy tone. Roberta Maxwell was a woman his mom had been shoving at him ever since Kelly had disappeared.

Though his mother had never come out and said I told you so, she didn't have to. It was there as plain as if she'd hung a banner.

She'd never approved of Kelly. Never liked that Ryan was marrying her. She'd been polite, though. Ryan had demanded it of her. He wouldn't allow any of his family to disrespect the woman he'd chosen to be his wife.

After what had happened with Jarrod and Kelly, he'd expected his mother to be more smug; but she'd been oddly sympathetic. The last thing he wanted at the moment, though, was to bring Kelly to an awkward dinner where his mom would sit with that pinched look on her face and Jarrod would say God knows what.

He'd wondered what would happen when the inevitable confrontation with Jarrod occurred.

Now he knew, and it hadn't gone at all as he'd imagined.

"I think we'll do dinner another time. Kelly and I aren't up to it at the moment."

He said his goodbyes and hung up, starting the car and slamming it into Reverse. He needed some distance before he went off the deep end.

He drove aimlessly and ended up at his office building before he even realized that he was heading in that direction. He didn't often drive, and usually only when he was leaving the city. He kept his car parked and used his car service. But today he hadn't been in any mood to wait for pickup.

He parked and went up to his office, acknowledging Jansen's look of surprise since he'd just told his assistant that morning that he wouldn't be in for several days.

He waved off Jansen's question of whether or not he needed anything and shut the door to his office. Then he flopped into his chair and swiveled around to stare out the window.

The weather had turned cold and gray, much more suited to his mood. After spending several days in Texas, where it was a good deal warmer, even in winter, coming back to the cold of the Northeast was a bit of an adjustment.

His cell phone rang, and he almost didn't answer. It was Cam, and Cam would want to know what had prompted his departure from Moon Island. Ryan was supposed to fly back to New York with Cam and Devon but he'd left in a hurry with a flimsily uttered excuse.

Deciding not to delay the inevitable, he put the phone to his ear.

"You and Dev make it back?"

"There you are. Been trying to call you for the past twenty-four hours. Where the hell did you go in such a hurry?" Cam demanded.

Ryan sighed. "My investigator called. He found Kelly." There was dead silence and then he heard Cam murmuring to someone else. Probably Dev.

"And?" Cam finally said.

"She was in Houston. I left the island to go and see if it was her."

"And?" Cam asked again.

"It was. I brought her back to New York with me."

"You did *what?* Why the hell did you do that?"

Ryan sighed at the incredulity in Cam's voice. And then because he needed to unload on someone, he said, "She's pregnant, Cam."

"Oh, Christ. What is with all the pregnant women showing up? I'll ask you the same question I asked Rafael when Bryony appeared out of nowhere. How do you know it's yours?"

"I don't believe I said it was mine," Ryan said mildly. "What I said was that she's pregnant."

"Uh-huh, and you'd just bring your ex-fiancée back to New York with you because she's pregnant with someone else's baby?"

"Don't be a smart-ass. The thing is, it *could* be my baby. Or it could be my brother's. Are you seeing my problem now?"

"Man, I'd say you have a whole hell of a lot of problems that I'm glad I don't have. What does she say about all of this?"

"That's just it. She's pissed. At me. She acts like I've wronged her. I don't get it. She hasn't said whose baby it is. She hasn't denied that it's my child but neither has she confirmed that it's mine."

"Has it ever occurred to you that she doesn't know?" Cam asked dryly.

Ryan scowled and then pinched the bridge of his nose between his fingers.

"Sorry, man, it had to be said. If she was sleeping with you and your brother plus God knows who else, she probably doesn't have a clue who the baby daddy is."

"God, stop with the snark. You're giving me a headache. Kelly isn't some whore."

"I never said she was."

"You implied it."

"Look, you're getting pissed at the wrong person here. I'm just asking—as a friend—whether you've lost your everloving mind. But then again, I thought you were insane for hiring an investigator to find her. Well, you found her and now you have to deal with the fallout. I'll tell you just what I told Rafael when he was faced with similar issues. Call your lawyer. Get paternity testing done."

"I don't want it to come to that," Ryan said quietly. "Damn it, I just want to know what went wrong." He broke off and shook his head. This was a pointless conversation to be having. Cam was an unforgiving bastard on his best day. As soon as he heard what Kelly had done, he'd basically written her off. Cam might be a hard-ass but he was a loyal hard-ass.

Cam was silent for a moment. "Look man, I'm sorry. I get that this has you tied in knots. Personally, I think you ought to go out, have a few drinks and get laid. Come off that self-imposed celibacy stint you've been on since you threw her out. But I know you won't so I won't go there."

Ryan laughed and shook his head.

"Dev wants to talk to you a minute so hang on."

"See ya," Ryan muttered to empty air.

A second later, Dev came on the phone.

"I won't repeat all Cam has said other than to ditto everything. What I wanted to tell you is that I'll be out of pocket for a while."

"Oh? Eloping with Ashley?"

Dev muttered a not-so-nice directive and Ryan chuckled.

"No, there's an issue with the construction and we've already suffered so many delays on this project that I don't want to risk any more. I'm going down there myself. It'll be quicker than conference calls and playing phone tag."

Ryan frowned and then leaned back in his chair. "How soon were you planning to leave?"

"Day after tomorrow. I'd go sooner, but I can't. And Cam is going to be out of the country starting tomorrow and I can't very well ask Rafe to leave his honeymoon."

"Ah. So really you and Cam were calling to see if I'd do it."

"Well, yeah, but after hearing what's on your plate, I'll go. I can break away after tomorrow."

Ryan thought a moment and then made a split-second decision. "No, I'll go."

"Whoa. Wait a minute. I thought you had Kelly with you. A pregnant Kelly."

"Yeah, I do. I'll take her with me. It'll be perfect. It'll give us time away from… It'll give us some time alone to sort things out."

Ryan could hear Dev sigh all the way through the phone.

"You honestly want her back? After everything that's happened?"

Ryan gripped the phone and stared out his window. "I don't know yet. I need some answers before I make that kind of decision. But if she's pregnant with my baby, I'm not letting her go again."

"Okay, you go. I'll email you all the issues. Just keep me posted and let me know if you have problems. I can be there at a moment's notice."

"Will do. Look, I know you and Cam think I'm nuts, but I appreciate you having my back."

Dev's dry response was immediate. "Yeah, you're nuts. But whatever makes you happy, man."

Ryan hung up and stared at the phone for a long moment before summoning Jansen. He gave him a list of instructions, starting with the need for Kelly to see an obstetrician immediately. She'd need a doctor's clearance to travel, but if the doctor gave the okay, he planned for them to spend a few days alone. And maybe they could start putting the pieces back together.

Then he started a shopping list, ignoring Jansen's grimace. Kelly needed outfitting from head to toe.

Five

Kelly sat cross-legged on her bed, staring into empty space. She couldn't stay here. She'd been stupid to think that she could exist in an environment where she was exposed to Jarrod.

It had been all she could do to keep it together. She was furious that she'd sat there while that bastard stood in the doorway with his bewildered look of innocence, but she'd been paralyzed the moment he'd walked into Ryan's apartment.

She hated the feeling of helplessness and she'd never, *never* allow herself to be such a passive respondent again. Going forward, if she saw the bastard, she'd kick his ass, pregnant or not. And then she'd tell Ryan precisely what he could do with his precious brother.

She hated Jarrod with a passion she reserved for few things in her life. And she *hated* Ryan for turning his back on her when she absolutely needed him the most.

No, she couldn't stay here. Not a minute longer.

She forced herself to consider her alternatives. This time she wasn't fleeing on ragged impulse without caring which way the wind blew her. No, she would come up with a solid plan of action. She'd go someplace quiet and safe—a good place to raise her son or daughter.

"You're leaving, aren't you?"

Ryan's voice came from the door. She started guiltily and finally raised her eyes to his. Angry because she allowed herself to feel guilt even for a second, she hardened her gaze as she stared back at him.

"There's no reason for me to stay."

"Come with me into the living room," he said, holding his hand out to her. For a long moment she simply stared at his outstretched hand. She should refuse, but something in his voice made her comply and she slipped her hand into his much larger one. He pulled her up from the bed and led her into the living room.

Sitting on the couch, he pulled her down beside him. He ran an agitated hand through his hair. "I've been an ass and I'm sorry. You're in no condition to bear this stress and pressure and I've only added to your burden."

She opened her mouth to speak and he placed a finger over her lips. "Let me finish. I've been in the office all morning and I've got some problems arising with an extremely important project that my partners are unable to attend to. Problems that require my immediate attention and presence. I want you to come with me."

She stared blankly at him. Why? She didn't get it. Why torture themselves? Why was he so persistent in flogging the dead horse that was their relationship? He'd been the one to end it. He had rendered judgment and tossed her aside like she'd never meant anything to him.

She opened her mouth to ask him just that, but again, he silenced her with his finger.

"Let me take care of you, Kelly. Let's forget

for the time being all the problems in the past and just concentrate on the present."

"You can't be serious."

"I'm very serious. I've never been more serious in my life. We have a lot to work out. We can't do that if we aren't willing to spend the time together and talk."

She'd never wanted to break down and cry more in her entire life. If only he'd been willing to listen *before.* If only he'd been willing to talk, to understand *then.* The one person she should have been able to count on above all others had coldly looked through her and called her a liar. And now he wanted to kiss and make up?

He touched her face with his fingers, and she was surprised that they trembled against her skin. His eyes were imploring her and she wavered on the edge of indecision. God, was she actually contemplating this farce? Even as she posed the question to herself she was shaking her head in automatic refusal.

He stopped the negative sway of her head by cupping her cheek and stroking his thumb lightly over her lips.

"No pressure, no promises, no obligations. Just you and me and a restful week on the beach. It's a start. It's all I'm asking for. I'll only ask for what you're willing to give."

"But the baby—"

"I would never do anything to endanger the baby," he said quietly. "Or you. You'll have to see the doctor here and get his okay to travel. It's the only way I would consider taking you on this trip."

Her eyes dropped to her hands knotted in her lap. It was tempting, so very tempting. He was asking, not demanding, and for a moment she was transported back to their time together—to the wonderfully tender and caring Ryan she had been engaged to. Could she leave him again after spending a week with him? Because she had no future with a man who could so coldly discard their relationship over the word of another.

The silence stretched out between them as she grappled with the decision. Yes, she would do it. She wasn't sure why. Nothing could come of it, but she wanted this time with him before she left to get on with her life. She nodded her assent and relief was stark in Ryan's eyes. It was so easy to pretend he cared when he put on such a good act. But clearly he didn't. If he had, they would still be together, married, awaiting the birth of their first child.

"We have to get you to the doctor this afternoon for a checkup. If he gives the thumbs-up we'll fly out tomorrow, so it's important you get plenty of rest today and tonight. Once we get there, the most strenuous thing you'll have to do is walk from the hotel room to the beach."

"I want separate rooms," she said.

"I've reserved us a suite."

She frowned but didn't argue.

"You won't regret this, Kell," he said, reverting to his pet name for her. She had the strangest urge to weep. How had they gotten so far away from the plans they had made just months earlier?

"We can do this. We can work it out."

She closed her eyes. The thing was, it was easy to be seduced by the intensity in those words. But going forward would be impossible until they'd addressed their past. And she never ever wanted to go back to that horrible day when her world had been so brutally upended.

The doctor was very approving of a week of rest and relaxation for Kelly and cautioned her to seek medical attention if the swelling got worse or she developed other symptoms.

Ryan had hung on to every word the doctor said and had acted just like a concerned husband and father. Instead of making her feel good, it depressed the hell out of her because it drew attention to the fact that their situation was hopeless.

When they arrived back at the apartment there were several department store bags stacked just inside the door. She eyed them curiously because they were decidedly feminine-looking, and if she wasn't mistaken, there was even a bag from a well-known lingerie store.

She glanced at Ryan, one eyebrow arched in question.

"Oh good, Jansen's been by," Ryan said as he walked over to the assortment of bags. "They're for you. For our trip." He gathered the handles and brought everything over to the couch, gesturing for her to have a look.

A little befuddled, she opened the packages, finding several maternity sundresses and sleek designer outfits, as well as beach attire all the way to a pair of sandals. As suspected, there were even all the girlie accoutrements in the lingerie bag.

"You shouldn't have done this," she murmured. How quickly they had fallen back into their old routine, and her discomfort level was off the charts.

"*I* didn't," he replied. "Jansen went shopping for me."

Despite herself, she smiled at the image of Ryan's hunky assistant traipsing through the maternity department in search of clothes and—even more hilarious—going into the lingerie store to buy panties and bras.

"How is Jansen?"

"Fine," Ryan replied. "Same as ever."

"Thank you for this," she added, swallowing her all-important pride for the moment.

His smile was genuine. "You're quite welcome.

Why don't you go lie down for a while and I'll pack our suitcases. Then we can have dinner. We'll call it an early night since we're leaving tomorrow morning."

She left the clothes on the couch and slowly rose. It was stupid of her to soften toward him. It was stupid to wish even for a moment that things were back to the way they'd been before.

But being stupid didn't stop the yearning deep inside her aching heart. Sadness overwhelmed her, and she hurriedly left the living room so he wouldn't see her tears.

The next morning Ryan gently shook her awake and she stretched languidly before getting up. After her shower, he fixed them breakfast. When they were done eating, he gathered their luggage to take down to the car.

On the drive to the airport Kelly was quiet. A part of her felt a tingle of excitement at the prospect of a week in paradise with Ryan, while the other part dreaded the forced intimacy. She had focused so much on her anger and hatred that it had come as a shock to her that she was still deeply in love with Ryan. And that frustrated her more than anything. Was she a masochist?

First of all to love a man who quite obviously did not love her in return, but to love him even after his most cutting betrayal? Pathetic.

To her surprise, they weren't taking a commercial flight. Ryan had chartered a private jet to take them nonstop to the island.

The flight was just a few hours, but halfway through she began fidgeting in her seat. She was nervous, edgy, and she was suffering a major case of cold feet.

"Why don't you recline your seat," he said, reaching over to help her.

When she was tilted back he nudged her over. "Turn on your side and I'll rub your back."

Too uncomfortable to turn down his touch, she faced the window and settled on her side.

Strong, tender fingers began a slow exploration of her back, rubbing and kneading. She sighed in contentment and relief as the tension faded in her muscles. Yawning widely, she snuggled deeper into the seat, enjoying the delicious sensations his touch was bringing.

For just a little while, she forced the past from her mind. She forced thoughts of the future away as well. All she focused on was the fact that she was with Ryan and he was acting as tender and loving as he had when they'd been together.

She went to sleep with a smile on her face.

As they prepared to land, Ryan shook her awake and raised her seat back up. She was so relaxed and lethargic that she sat there quietly while the plane touched down.

Fifteen minutes later, Ryan wrapped a protective arm around her as they exited the plane. He seated her in the waiting car while he saw that the luggage was loaded and then they drove away.

They checked into the lavish hotel that was situated directly on the beach, and Ryan jokingly informed her that when his partnership's resort was built, it would make the one they were staying in look like a two-star hotel instead of the five stars it boasted.

Kelly found that hard to believe when they were ushered into a sprawling suite that was many times bigger than her apartment in Houston.

She sank into the couch, that looked out the sliding patio doors to the private expanse of beach beyond. Ryan put away their luggage and then knelt in front of her, slipping her shoes off to inspect her feet for swelling. He began massaging the souls, moving up to the instep and arch. A moan of absolute pleasure escaped her lips.

"Feel good?"

"Oh my God, does it."

He continued his ministrations, watching her silently. Her hand crept to her rounded belly and she smiled as the baby rolled beneath her fingers.

"Is the baby moving?" Ryan asked.

She nodded and he stopped rubbing her feet.

"Can I feel?"

She brought his hand to her stomach and placed it over the spot where her hand had been. He jerked in surprise as her stomach bumped beneath his palm, and his expression was akin to awe.

"That's incredible. Doesn't it hurt?"

Chuckling, she said, "No. It isn't always comfortable, but it's certainly not painful."

He kept his hand there a few more moments and then rose, a regretful glint in his eyes. "Would you like to have dinner on the patio or do you want to go eat in the restaurant?"

"Here, please," she replied. "I like our view and it's private."

He nodded his agreement and went to phone in their room service order.

Thirty minutes later the meal was wheeled in on a serving cart and the attendant set the table out on the patio. The two ate in silence, enjoying the setting sun and the sound of the waves crashing in the distance.

As they finished, Ryan suggested she go to bed; but she wasn't tired. She was quite rested actually and felt an eagerness to explore their secluded cove. When she expressed the desire to take a walk along the beach, Ryan hesitated at first, but agreed to accompany her when she was adamant about going.

Kelly breathed deeply of the salty air as the ocean breeze whipped at her long hair, lifting it from her waist. She slipped her sandals off and bent awkwardly to pick them up. Ryan quickly gathered them for her and tucked them under his arm. Digging her toes into the damp sand, she ventured into the bubbling surf, letting the foam wash over her feet.

Ryan removed his shoes and joined her after he rolled up the cuffs of his jeans. He slipped an arm around her as they made their way down the beach, but she resisted the urge to move closer to his side.

"We shouldn't go far," he cautioned. "You aren't supposed to be on your feet for this long. I promised the doctor this would be a restful trip for you."

"This is a lot more restful than being on my feet twelve hours a day," she said lightly.

He frowned and his hand tightened around her waist. "That won't happen again."

She didn't respond, but turned back toward their suite. Ryan's hand slipped from her waist as she walked ahead of him. When they walked back inside the patio doors, Kelly sank onto the plush couch.

"Would you like something to drink?" he asked.

"Juice, if you have it."

He rummaged in the well-stocked fridge and came back with a glass of orange juice a moment later.

"You should go on to bed," he said gently. "There'll be plenty of time to explore the beach after you've had a good night's rest."

Even though she was tired, the day had been so…perfect…that she hated to bring it to an end. Spending the time with Ryan had been bittersweet, a throwback to happier times when things had been…

She sighed. She had to stop with the endless string of memories. She had a week with Ryan. One week when the past wasn't supposed to matter. If he could forget then she would try to as well. And when it came to an end, maybe her memories of him wouldn't be quite so bitter.

She struggled to get out of the ultrasoft couch and laughed when she realized she was well and truly stuck. Ryan reached down to help her to her feet and she finally managed to stand.

For a long moment she stood in front of him, her gaze stroking softly over the chiseled lines of his face. It was the first time she'd allowed herself to stare unguardedly at him.

"Good night, Ryan," she whispered softly.

He looked as though he wanted to kiss her and for a moment she wondered how she would react if he did. But finally he said, "Good night, Kelly. Sleep well."

She turned to go into her bedroom, little twinges of regret nagging her the entire way.

Six

Kelly didn't sleep that night. Not that it should have come as any surprise to her. She lay awake in her bed, reliving the past. The first time she met Ryan. How he'd swept her off her feet and into a passionate and all-consuming relationship.

From the day he first asked her out, they hadn't spent a single day apart for several weeks. By the end of the first month, she'd moved into his apartment, and by the end of the second month of their whirlwind courtship, his ring was on her finger.

She had never been quite sure why he'd chosen her. It wasn't as if she thought she was inferior, but Ryan Beardsley was an extremely wealthy man. He could have his pick of women. Why Kelly?

She didn't have family connections. She didn't have money or prestige. She was a simple college student eking out a living on a waitress's salary.

Until Ryan.

Everything had changed for her, and maybe she'd been too caught up in the fairy tale that was her relationship with Ryan to ever question the important things. Like whether he loved and trusted her.

How would he react now if once again she tried to tell him what had really happened the day he'd tossed her out of his life? He hadn't believed her then. Why would now be any different?

Tears blurred her vision as her thoughts drifted back to that day.

Kelly stared at the pregnancy test, a mixture of joy and worry bubbling through her chest. She quickly hid the stick and then smiled as she imagined telling Ryan the news. She didn't think he'd be upset. They were planning to marry soon and they'd often talked of their desire to start a family.

She couldn't wait to tell him. She searched her memory for what he had going on at the office today. He didn't have any important meetings and he was supposed to be in his office for the entirety of the afternoon. That meant she could pop in and surprise him.

She hugged herself in excitement, nearly dancing across the floor of their bedroom as she imagined his reaction.

A noise from the living room halted her. Then she smiled. Oh, this would be perfect. Ryan was home. He sometimes surprised her by dropping in for lunch. Today his timing was impeccable.

She started to call out to him when Jarrod, appeared in the doorway to the bedroom.

She was momentarily speechless. While Jarrod popped in frequently, he always did so when Ryan was at home. He had to know Ryan was working today.

"Jarrod, what are you doing here? Ryan's at work. I don't expect him home until later."

"I came to talk to you," Jarrod said.

She cocked her head to the side. "Okay. What's up? Let's go into the living room."

He ignored her and took another step into the bedroom. Unease prickled down her spine. Something was definitely off with him.

"How much would it take for you to walk away from Ryan?"

Her eyes widened in shock. She couldn't have heard him correctly. "Excuse me?"

"Don't play dumb. You're a smart girl. How much would it take for you to dump Ryan and take off?"

"You're offering me money? Did your mother put you up to this? You're both out of your minds. I love Ryan. He loves me. We're getting married."

Something that looked like genuine regret flickered across Jarrod's face. He fidgeted nervously and then pinned her with his stare. "I'd hoped you'd make this easy. It's not a small amount of money we're offering."

The "we" in that statement confirmed Kelly's suspicions that Ryan's mother was indeed the mastermind of this operation. She was about to tell Jarrod exactly where he and his mother could get off when he took another step toward her. The look in his eyes had her hastily backing away.

"I think you should go now," she said even as she reached for the phone.

Jarrod lunged across the bed, knocking the phone from her hand. She was so stunned by the sudden attack that for a moment she didn't—couldn't—defend herself.

He shoved her down on the bed, his hands moving roughly over her body, pushing at her shirt, pulling at her pants. She drew her knee up, trying to catch him in the groin, but he dodged and then rolled her underneath him.

She cried out in pain at the rough mauling. She was furious and terrified. He fully intended to rape her in Ryan's bed. Had he lost his mind? Ryan would kill him for this.

His hands moved over her skin with bruising force. Knowing if she wasn't able to fight him off that he'd assault her in her own home, she began struggling with renewed force.

She finally managed to land a blow between his legs, which had him doubling over, clutching at himself. She rolled, falling to the floor, her hands desperately grabbing at her clothing.

She got to her feet, her hand clutching her bruised throat. "He'll kill you for this," she gasped. "How did you think you'd get away with it? My God, you're his brother! You bastard."

She started for the door, her only thought to get to Ryan, but Jarrod's words gave her pause.

"He'll never believe you."

"You're insane," she choked out even as she ran for the door.

But Jarrod had been right. Ryan hadn't believed her. Jarrod had called his brother from Ryan's own apartment before she could arrive at Ryan's office. He'd given Ryan his own accounting of what happened, and the genius of his story was that he told Ryan exactly what Kelly would tell him. Only Jarrod told Ryan that Kelly had been the instigator and that when Jarrod told her he was going to tell Ryan that Kelly had cheated on him, Kelly concocted a smug story that Jarrod had assaulted her.

Jarrod played his part to the hilt. That he *was the victim of Kelly's lies and manipulations. So when Kelly ran to Ryan's office and related the exact story that Jarrod warned Ryan she would tell, Ryan had been coldly furious.*

He'd written her that damn check and he'd thrown her out of his life.

Kelly lay in her bed, numbed by the painful memories. And now, here on this island, she was supposed to forget the past. Put it behind her. Move forward and pick up where she and Ryan had left off.

Forgetting that she'd been horribly betrayed by people she trusted.

When Ryan knocked softly at her door, she roused herself from the weight of her thoughts, cursing that it was already morning and she'd done little better than catnap.

She struggled out of bed and hauled her robe around her body then staggered to the door to open it.

Ryan stood outside, dressed in slacks and a

dress shirt. He had impending business written all over him.

"I've left breakfast on the bar for you. I have to run out to the construction site for a few hours. Will you be all right alone?"

She nodded, relieved that she wouldn't immediately have to face him. She needed time to regain her composure. Time to mentally reconstruct her defenses.

"Yes, of course. When will you be back?"

He checked his watch. "It's eight now. I shouldn't be later than noon. We can have lunch in the hotel restaurant and then go for a walk on the beach if you like. Take it easy while I'm gone. I'll worry if I know you're on the beach by yourself."

She rolled her eyes. "I think I'm capable of leaving the hotel room alone."

"I know you are," he said quietly. "I just worry and I'd prefer to be with you."

There wasn't much she could say to that, so she nodded. "I'll see you at lunch."

He lifted his hand in a wave and then walked

away. For a moment she stared after him and then she closed the door, leaning against it.

Day one of attempting to forget the past and forge ahead.

"How's that working out for you?" she muttered as she traipsed into the bathroom.

Though she had every intention of at least taking in the portion of the beach right outside the patio of her suite, she still wanted a long, hot bath. Even if it meant she'd still have to shower when she came in with sand in all her nooks and crannies.

After drawing a tub full of steaming water, she sank up to her ears and sighed in complete bliss. She hadn't made the water too hot, and she wouldn't stay long. Then she'd go bake in the sun for a bit.

After twenty minutes, regretfully, she toed the lever for the drain and then hauled herself out of the tub. Her stomach growled and she hurriedly went through the motions of dressing and putting on enough makeup to look presentable in public.

She devoured the bagel, the cinnamon roll and

the fruit Ryan had left for her. She ate every crumb and licked her fingers, feeling like a pig, but a very satisfied pig. It had been a while since she'd had a hearty appetite and it had been weeks since anything had actually tasted good to her.

After downing an entire glass of juice, she smacked her lips in pleasure and went in search of a beach towel she could spread out on the sand.

She'd seen umbrellas dotting the private section of the beach reserved for the hotel guests and she planned to make good use of one while she waited for Ryan to return.

After months of being on her feet for hours on end, working a thankless job for paltry wages, a day lounging on the beach sounded about as decadent as it got. She was going to enjoy every minute.

She didn't bother with sandals since she wasn't going far. The sand felt luxurious beneath her feet. So warm and soft. She sighed in contentment as she headed for one of the nearby umbrellas.

The sound of the ocean filled her ears, beautiful and so peaceful. Here was a place where she could forget the pain of her past. It was a place made for being soothed. A vacation for the soul.

It sounded ridiculous and a little corny but she liked it and quickly adopted it as her motto for this trip.

She spread the towel out over the sand, positioned the umbrella just so and then sank down, drawing her knees up as she stared over the rolling waves.

Closing her eyes, she inhaled deeply and enjoyed the breeze dancing across her face. Her sleepless night quickly caught up to her as tight muscles relaxed and the tension she'd held for so long gradually fell away.

Soon it was hard to keep her eyes open, so she stretched out on the towel and turned on her side to face the ocean. The umbrella provided plenty of shade. A nap was too tempting to pass up. She'd simply wait for Ryan here.

Shortly after noon, Ryan let himself into the room and looked around for Kelly. He called out to her but got no answer. He checked the bedroom in case she was napping, but found that the maid service had already come through to make the beds.

He sighed, knowing she hadn't paid the least bit of attention to his concern over her going onto the beach without him. It wasn't as if he thought anything would happen to her or that she was incapable of being alone, but her medical condition concerned him. And yeah, he was probably being a little overprotective, but he found with Kelly—just as he always had—he tended to overreact.

He stepped out onto the patio and scanned the beach, looking for any sign of her. When he didn't immediately spot her, he began walking toward the umbrellas that dotted the sand.

When he got to the third, he saw her lying on her side, eyes closed and looking so damn beautiful—and vulnerable—that it made his chest ache.

He watched the soft rise and fall of her chest. The mound of her belly moved in a ripple across the floral sarong she wore. Her feet were bare and he could still detect signs of swelling around her ankles.

It wasn't as bad as it had been, but it still concerned him a great deal.

He eased down onto the towel beside her and stroked his hand through her silky blond hair. He slid his fingers down her arm, over the curve of her hip and then down to the tight ball of her belly.

She sighed in her sleep and shifted closer to his hand. The urge to pull her into his arms was so strong that he jerked his hand away so he wouldn't do just that.

If only he could erase the past six months and have things back the way they were. But now he had to deal with not only Kelly's betrayal, but the fact that she carried his child. Whether she admitted it or not he felt strongly that she carried *his* baby. He wouldn't allow himself to think otherwise.

Reaching out, he shook her, not wanting her to be exposed to the midday rays of sun, umbrella or not. She came awake slowly and blinked sleepily at him. Her soft smile of pleasure warmed him to his toes.

"When did you get back?" she asked in a groggy, sleep filled voice.

"A few minutes ago," he said, smiling at her. "Are you ready to go eat?"

She nodded and pushed herself up. He reached down to help her up, and she slid her fingers into his, allowing him to pull her to her feet. Wrapping his arm around her shoulders, he guided her back to the suite, enjoying the few moments of intimacy afforded him.

While she showered and changed, he called Devon to give him an update on the construction schedule. The two men talked for a few minutes and Dev didn't mention Kelly once. Something Ryan was glad for.

No matter that his friends and his family thought he was crazy, this was something he simply had to do. He hadn't been able to stop thinking about Kelly in the months since their relationship had ended. He might be the biggest fool in the world, but he was determined to figure this out between them. Even if it meant eventually going their separate ways.

When Kelly reemerged from her room, there was a lightness to her eyes that had been absent ever since he'd found her in the café in Houston. She looked a lot like the old Kelly. The Kelly he'd been crazy about. The one who always had a ready smile, was quick to laugh and who offered her affection freely.

The reserved, angry Kelly was someone he didn't know.

She seemed a little nervous and unsure as she came to stand by the bar, and he hated that there was a tangible barrier between them. Before she wouldn't have hesitated to launch herself into his arms and give him one of her big, squeezing hugs.

Now? He ached to get close enough to her that she didn't withdraw.

"You ready?" he asked, forcing a casual note into his voice.

She nodded. He put his hand to her back, noting the expanse of flesh bared by the sundress. Jansen had done well. The dress fit her like a dream, molding in all the right places. The bodice was held up by ends tied at the nape of her neck; but her flesh was bare all the way down to the small of her back.

Where his palm rested, he itched to caress and stroke until she responded to him, until he proved that the attraction between them hadn't died.

They walked down to the restaurant that overlooked the ocean and were seated in a private alcove that had a huge glass window, giving them an unobstructed view of the beach.

As they looked over their menus, Ryan stole a glance at Kelly. Seeming to sense his perusal, she looked up and offered a tentative smile. He smiled back, captivated by the sparkle in her blue eyes.

She was…beautiful. And this time when she looked at him, he didn't see the dark anger that had sparked so often since their reunion.

The moment came to a shrieking halt a second later.

"Ryan! What are you doing here?"

The feminine voice rang out over the secluded

area, making him wince and Kelly jump in surprise. He glanced up to see Roberta Maxwell bearing down on their table and he muttered an appropriate expletive under his breath.

As she approached the table, he rose to return her greeting. He brushed a polite kiss over her cheek when she presented it to him and tried to extricate his hand from hers when she grabbed on to it.

"I'm here on business. The question is, what are *you* doing here?"

Her laughter tinkled out like fine china. "Oh, this is one of my favorite places to visit. The food is just divine, and the accommodations can't be beat." She turned to Kelly who was eyeing Roberta warily. "Who is this, Ryan?"

Like hell she didn't know who Kelly was and like hell she just happened to be here. He'd lay odds that Roberta Maxwell had never been to St. Angelo in her life. She was shockingly transparent and didn't seem to give a damn. That could only mean she was here to cause trouble. His mother's name was written all over this and he was so furious he wanted to strangle Roberta's skinny neck. And then move on to his mother. He never should have informed his mother that he'd be out of town and he damn sure shouldn't have told her *where* he was going. He'd hoped… Well, it didn't really matter what he'd hoped. Roberta was here and it was apparent it wasn't some damn coincidence.

"Roberta, meet Kelly Christian. Kelly, this is an acquaintance of mine, Roberta Maxwell."

Roberta's smile was dazzling and she playfully fluttered her fingers at Ryan. "Oh la, darling. Surely I rate higher than an acquaintance."

Kelly's eyes narrowed and Ryan decided that politeness was overrated.

"We're having a private dinner, Roberta. If you'll excuse us, please?"

Undaunted, Roberta entwined her arm in his and her voice dropped to a low purr. "We must get together while you are here. Perhaps have dinner ourselves. I was so sorry to have missed you the last time I had dinner with your mother. I do love her so."

He extricated himself from her grasp and stepped back a few paces from her. "I'm afraid my time here is spoken for," he said. "Perhaps when we return to New York, Kelly and I can have you over for dinner." He said the last pointedly, not that he really expected it to deter Roberta. It wasn't his fault she was as thick as a brick.

Roberta's eyes flashed with annoyance and her finely painted lips formed a full pout. "Really, darling, when did you decide to take back the little cheater?"

Kelly's face blanched and she threw down her napkin. Ryan's hand shot up to silence Roberta. "You know, I've had about enough. It's time you left. Give my *regards* to my mother, and while you're at it, tell her to stay the hell out of my affairs. Advice you'd be well advised to take as well."

She twisted her pouty lips and ran a well-manicured set of nails down the lapel of his suit. "No need to get huffy, darling. I know you have to be polite to her since you don't know whose baby she carries."

With a careless wave, she walked gracefully away, leaving Ryan so furious that he wanted to hurl his chair across the room. But his anger had nothing on the fury flashing in Kelly's eyes when he turned to see her standing in front of her seat, her fists clenched and pressed to the top of the table.

Seven

Ryan gripped the back of his seat with one hand and ran a hand through his hair with the other. "I'm sorry."

"I've lost my appetite," she stated flatly as she pushed away from her seat.

"Kelly, don't," he protested. "You have to eat. Don't let that cat ruin our dinner."

Her lips tightened in fury. "That *cat* seems to know an awful lot about our situation, wouldn't you agree?"

She turned from the table and stalked toward the entrance of the restaurant. As soon as she hit the lobby, she turned down the long corridor leading to their suite. Angrily, she jammed the card into the lock, swearing when the light didn't immediately flash green. She slammed the card in again and yanked at the handle when the telltale whir sounded.

Once inside, she bolted the door behind her and went into her bedroom. She perched on the edge of the bed, and in the distance she heard knocking and then Ryan's angry voice through the door.

She was too angry to give a damn that he'd have to walk all the way around to the patio glass doors to gain entrance.

She'd had enough of this farcical…hell, she didn't even know what to call it this time around. Whatever it was, she wanted out.

It was enough that she'd been humiliated by Ryan and his brother, but now she had to put up with some brainless airhead piling on as well? They could all go to hell.

Her head came up when her bedroom door flew open, revealing a livid Ryan. Yeah, well he wasn't the only one, and she wasn't backing down. She got to her feet and faced him head-on.

"What the hell is wrong with you, Kelly? It isn't like you to go to such extremes. What do you hope to accomplish by locking me out? Ignoring our problems isn't going to make them go away."

"How would you know what isn't like me?" she retorted. "It would seem you never knew me at all."

His eyes flashed and he nodded. "That much is certainly true."

Pissed at the innuendo in his response, she fixed him with a cold stare. "I want out of here. I want the first flight out I can get. This is ridiculous. It's a waste of time. It's never going to work between us, Ryan."

He swore and moved to stand just in front of her, his hands gripping her shoulders. "We had an agreement. One week together and we forget the past."

She gaped at him incredulously. "Did you not witness that debacle in the restaurant? How on earth would she know so much about me and our relationship unless *you* told her? How the hell are we supposed to forget the past when your little floozy is busy throwing it in my face? I don't appreciate being made a fool of. And I certainly don't appreciate being bandied about in conversation like yesterday's garbage."

"I never discussed you with her," he said emphatically.

"Amazing then that she knew so much."

"Why is it you have so little faith in me, Kelly? *I* didn't betray *you.*"

She flinched. It always came back to this. No matter what, it always came back to the fact that he believed she had betrayed him and refused to entertain any other possibility.

She turned away from him, trying to control the tide of rage boiling over her. Shaking with her attempts to tamp down her angry shouts, she clenched her hands and closed her eyes tightly.

Suddenly she was spun around to face him again and he crushed his lips to hers, cupping her face in his hands. She brought her hands up between them to push against his chest, but his arms went tightly around her back, pulling her even closer to him.

She moaned low in her throat as his kiss gentled and became exploratory. He moved her to the edge of the bed and lowered her onto the mattress, never ceasing his slow movement over her lips. "Damn it, Kelly, just don't say anything for a while. No words. We can't seem to have a conversation without hurting each other, so for just a little while let's communicate without talking."

She gazed into his eyes as he drew away from her and studied his expression. How could she want him so much after all the mistrust and hurt? His fingertips caressed her cheek and she closed her eyes, arching further into his hand.

What if she let him make love to her? Would it be so bad? Or would it just confirm his low opinion of her.

Like a bucket of ice water, that thought quashed any desire she had to surrender to his lovemaking. He must have sensed her withdrawal because he drew away, looking at her in confusion.

"I can't do this," she said, scrambling to sit up on the bed. "Not knowing what you think of me."

The words caught and raggedly slipped from

her lips. Drawing protective arms around her chest, she sat on the rumpled covers watching him warily.

"Don't stare at me like you expect me to pounce," he said in disgust. "I am not into unwilling women."

He left the room, slamming the door solidly behind him.

Feeling more alone than she had when she left him the first time, she edged off the bed and walked into the bathroom to splash cool water on her flushed face.

She stared back at her reflection and saw the utter misery in her eyes. Tears welled. Her chest hurt. Her heart hurt. This was no way to live.

She wouldn't beg him to believe her. She'd already done that. On her knees no less. What was left? He didn't believe her. She wasn't going to beg him again. There was nowhere for this relationship to go but straight to hell in a handbasket.

Turning the water off, she put her elbows on the countertop and buried her face in her hands as sobs billowed from her throat.

She hadn't been happy in six long months but now her misery was even more pronounced. Her circumstances hadn't been the best in Houston, but she hadn't had to look at the man she loved and know that he thought the worst of her.

Tears still sliding down her face, she went blindly back into the bedroom and curled into a ball on the bed. Her shoulders shook and the tears that she'd held back for so long streamed down her cheeks in steady trails.

After a few minutes, the bed dipped and Ryan put a hand to her cheek. "I'm sorry, Kell," he said hoarsely. "Don't cry. Please don't cry."

Gently he lifted her into his arms and cradled her to his chest. She clung to him and buried her face in his neck as her tears soaked into his shirt.

"I'm sorry. This isn't how I wanted things to go. I never meant to upset you or make you feel worthless. I swear it."

His voice was thick with regret and it trembled with emotion as he stroked his hand over her hair.

"You have to know that Roberta was here for the sole reason of causing trouble between us."

She went still against him, knowing that what she was about to say would probably only piss him off more, but she was through pulling her punches.

"Are you ready to admit that your mother hates me and would do anything to get rid of me? If you didn't talk to Roberta about us, then who the hell do you think did?"

"I know," he said quietly. "It won't work, though. As soon as we return home, I'll put an end to this. I promise. She won't be allowed to hurt you like this."

She sagged against him. She wanted so desperately to believe him this time. His eyes were slowly being opened. Did this mean he would eventually accept her version of what happened six months ago?

He pressed his lips to the top of her head and whispered softly. "Stay with me, Kelly. We have so much to work out. God knows we've been through a lot together. But in order to do that I need you here with me. Not a thousand miles away in some godforsaken hellhole where I can't take care of you and our baby."

He pulled her carefully away and wiped at the trails of wetness on her cheeks with his thumbs. His gaze was haunted, intense and dark with emotion. Honest to God, he looked like he was hurting every bit as much as she was.

It had been on the tip of her tongue to deny that he was the father yet again, but this time she didn't. It was pointless to argue with him, and besides, he *was* the father.

He too was obviously expecting her to deny it because when she remained silent his eyes lit with hope.

"Give us a chance, Kell. Let me take care of you and the baby. Whatever is wrong between us, we can fix it."

"I wish I had your optimism," she murmured. How to explain that their problems were insurmountable in the face of his lack of trust in her?

He lowered his lips to hers, kissing her so lovingly that she felt a resurgence of tears. She broke away and then laid her cheek against his chest. It felt so good to be back in his arms, for just a moment to let go of all the pain and resentment.

He put a hand to her hair, his touch tentative.

“Kell, we need to talk about the baby. But first we have to settle this matter between us.”

She closed her eyes, feeling dread settle in the pit of her stomach. “If I tell you the baby is yours, will you believe me?”

He went still against her and then he let all his breath out. He cupped his hand to the side of her face and held her against his chest.

“I’ll believe you, Kell.”

Slowly she pushed against his chest until she was eye level with him. How it hurt that he was willing to believe her now about their child, but he hadn’t been willing to believe her then when it came to his brother.

“She’s yours,” she said in a quiet voice.

Satisfaction was a savage light in his eyes. He framed her face tightly in his hands and then lowered his mouth to take hers in a possessive, fierce sweep.

Her lips were swollen when she managed to tear her mouth away. Her pulse raced and they stared at each other in silence. She was afraid to believe in him. So afraid she was nearly paralyzed with it.

"Do you believe me? I have to know, Ryan. We can't go forward unless you believe me."

His hand drifted down to the bulge of her belly and he slid his palm over the curve, splaying his fingers out until he covered a wide area.

"I believe you."

She bit her lip to keep from asking him if he'd believe her about everything else. She knew he didn't, he hadn't. And maybe it was too late. Wasn't it?

"Kelly?" His soft entreaty broke through her musings. He stroked her cheek with the tip of one finger. "I believe you. Okay? Jarrod said he wore a condom and the timing was right for us. I won't believe you slept with anyone else. It was just that one time with Jarrod, wasn't it?"

The soft plea froze her to the bone. Hurt crashed through her heart—a heart she thought was already irreparably shattered. She was wrong. She hadn't thought there was anything

Ryan could do to hurt her further. She'd been wrong about that too.

"Why does that make you cry?"

Ryan wiped at the tear that trailed down her cheek, his expression one of complete bewilderment. Then he leaned in and kissed the moisture away.

She braced her hands on his arms, her mind a chaotic twist of anger and wretched grief. It took every bit of her strength to gather her shattered composure and speak to him when what she wanted to do was flee.

"If this has any hope of working, you'll never breathe his name to me again. You were the one who wanted this. One week. No past. Forget the past. It's what you said. I'm holding you to it. You bring him up ever again, and I walk—no, I run. Are we clear?"

He looked shocked by her vehemence. He opened his mouth as if he wanted to push further, but she shook her head and started to slide from his lap.

He made a grab for her, pulling her close to him again. "All right. No past. I won't bring it up again. I promise. Will you stay, Kelly? Will you work with me?"

She closed her eyes again and the fight left her. Her head dropped down and exhaustion crept in, gripping the back of her neck, squeezing until her entire head ached vilely.

His fingers slid around her neck, rubbing and caressing with gentle pressure. Had she been that obvious?

"I still care about you, Kelly."

She leaned her forehead against his. His onslaught was relentless and he didn't play fair.

"I'm afraid," she whispered.

"So am I."

Surprised by his admission, she retreated a few inches and flicked her gaze up and down, searching for the truth in his eyes.

"Don't look at me like that. You aren't the only one hurting. I… Damn it, I promised we wouldn't bring the past up. I'm not going to. But you aren't the only one who got hurt in all this. I cared about you. I wanted to marry you. I…"

He dragged a hand through his hair. He suddenly looked haggard and tired, worn down by the dark emotion that flowed between the two of them.

"I still want to marry you," he quietly admitted.

Eight

The admission was stark, so plainly and painfully laid out. Almost as if he wasn't happy with the truth of the words but said them all the same. He stared at her, his discomfort growing by the second.

She stared back, baffled and unable to form a single-word response to his declaration.

He didn't love her. Didn't trust her. He believed the absolute worse about her. All he seemed willing to accept was that her child was his—and only because his brother had claimed to have worn a condom.

But he wanted to marry her.

She laughed.

It was a hysterical, shrill, unpleasant sound.

His eyes narrowed. "That wasn't exactly the reaction I'd hoped for."

Her own eyes widened. "Was that a proposal?"

She swallowed the laughter this time because he was wearing an extremely dark, agitated look.

He gripped the back of his neck. "No, yes, maybe. I'd like that to be where we end up. But we've got a long way to go before we get there. I just want you to say that you still care. Enough to want to stay and work things out. We'll take it slow. One day at a time. I won't let anything happen again like what happened at lunch."

"And how are you going to do that?" she asked softly. "How can you make your family or your acquaintances accept me? And they don't, Ryan. You always told me I imagined it, but let's be honest here. Your mother couldn't stand me. Your friends couldn't understand what you saw in me. And it's obvious your brother thought I was unfaithful. An opinion you adopted."

He rose abruptly. She slid off his lap and onto

the mattress as he stood by the bed, his hand still at his nape.

"You said you didn't want to talk about the past. Either we're going to or we aren't, but none of this pick and choose your shots."

He dropped his hand and then leaned over her, planting his hands on either side of her legs. "Just answer the question, Kelly. Are you going to stay? Do you even want to try? Are you willing to work this out so that maybe we can be happy together again?"

He asked it as though it was something she could answer immediately. It wasn't a simple matter. No matter which way she answered, she would be hurt.

She licked her lips. Her heart screamed at her that she was an idiot to get involved with him again. Her head told her that without trust their relationship was doomed from the start, and he'd already proved he had absolutely no faith in her.

Was she willing to put herself in a position where everyone else's word would be taken above her own?

But something deeper, beneath the pain and

the anger and the betrayal, stirred and twisted within her at the thought of being together with Ryan again.

She told herself that there was nothing wrong with staying with him until her child was born so she'd have a safe haven and a place to live. Food to eat. She'd have comfort. All the things she'd been denied for the past six months.

But she also knew she couldn't stay with him without involving her heart again. So the decision was whether she wanted to forgive and forget and move on or whether she wanted to make a clean, permanent break and move on, whatever that entailed.

Or maybe she should settle for a few stolen moments with a man she loved and hated with equal fervor.

The longer she was silent, the more the hope faded in Ryan's eyes. He seemed resigned to her inevitable rejection, and she couldn't help but draw the parallel between now and the time she'd stood so vulnerable in front of him, begging for his trust, his love, his support.

The idea of revenge didn't appeal. It left a

heavy feeling of sadness and brought her no happiness and certainly no peace.

She was a fool. And that too brought her no peace.

"I'll stay," she said in a voice devoid of the joy the decision should have brought.

Though it was lacking in her own tone and expression, hope flared back to life in Ryan's eyes. He gripped her arms and then slid his hands up over her shoulders and neck to gently hold her in place as he pressed a tender kiss to her lips.

There was a wealth of emotion conveyed in the simplest touch of his mouth. His breath came in ragged spurts from his chest and for the first time she realized how much he'd feared her rejection.

She wasn't a huge believer in karma but now she wondered if this was his penance. To feel as she had felt so many months before.

But that thought brought her no satisfaction either. She wouldn't wish that feeling on anyone.

He drew away and brushed the hair from her cheek and continued to stroke the contours of her face.

"Spend the afternoon with me, Kell. You need to eat. I'll order us food and we can go eat on the beach. Watch the sun go down. I had Jansen pack a bathing suit for you if you'd like to go in the water."

She reached for the hand that rested against her cheek and curled her fingers around it, holding it there for a long moment.

"I'd like that," she finally said.

She and Ryan strolled to the same umbrella she'd used for her nap earlier that morning and he spread out a blanket on the sand. After he was satisfied she would have a comfortable seat, he helped her down and then began unpacking the picnic basket prepared by the restaurant.

He settled beside her and they began to eat.

Kelly stared out over the water as she munched on one of the tasty little confections whose name escaped her. It had cheese and shrimp. She wasn't sure of the other ingredients, but it was good and she was starving.

The sky had started to soften. Wispy pastel tendrils flirted across the horizon as the sun sank lower. She closed her eyes and allowed the breeze to soothe her fried nerves.

She'd expended more emotional energy over the past months than she had in a lifetime. She wanted to exist free of distress. Just for a little while. She wanted to forget the nights she'd been unable to sleep for crying or the nights she'd lain awake hurting so much that she'd wondered if it would ever stop.

Here she just wanted to be. Here she could at least pretend that the past six months hadn't happened. This could very well have been her honeymoon. A romantic island getaway.

Ryan had certainly played the part of the solicitous husband.

"Penny for your thoughts?"

Slowly she dropped her gaze from the vivid splash of blue and turned her head to Ryan.

"I was thinking that it's easy to pretend here."

The blue in his eyes deepened until it ran darker than the water rolling onto shore.

"We could pretend," he acknowledged. "But we don't have to."

"So did you get things straightened out at the

building site?" she asked, not wanting to delve into pretend versus real. They were supposed to forget the past. At least for this week. That didn't leave a whole lot to talk about.

"Just a misunderstanding. I should have it cleared up by tomorrow. I have a joint meeting in the morning with the local contractors and the man we hired to oversee the project. If all goes well, I'll be finished and we'll have a few days to do what we want."

"When do you have to be back in New York?" she asked carefully. Because she knew the whole fantasy would come to a screeching halt once that happened.

"I don't know yet. I'm not in a hurry," he said as he studied her. "Right now I prefer to concentrate on the time we have here together."

She nodded, her acceptance coming a little easier now that she'd had more time to grasp the idea.

"Will you sleep with me tonight, Kelly?"

Her eyes widened.

He cursed. "That came out completely wrong. I'd like for us to sleep together. Actually sleep. In the same bed. I'd like to hold you again. Nothing more. Just let me hold you."

The idea of lying in his arms, of snuggling into his body and tangling her legs with his… It was so compelling that she suddenly wanted it more than her next breath.

Taking a deep breath, she nodded.

He reached over, took her hand and simply held it, their fingers wound tightly. He leaned back and positioned himself up on his elbow at an angle and then pulled her so she could rest against his chest.

They remained that way until hotel workers came out to light the torches along the beach as dusk deepened and the stars began to pop in the sky.

Soft music floated from down the beach where an outdoor lounge area was located. The notes with the waves made for incomparable music.

She leaned her head back in the crook of his neck and gazed dreamily up at the sky now that the umbrella had been folded down. He turned his face so that his lips brushed across her cheek in a kiss and then he too glanced skyward.

"Make a wish," she murmured.

"I have my wish. Now make yours."

She took a deep breath and held it for a long second. Then she closed her eyes and made her wish. Sadness crept in and took hold because she knew that some wishes couldn't come true.

After a moment, Ryan stirred under her and then carefully pushed her upward so he could move from behind her. He got to his feet, dusted sand from his jeans and reached down for her hand.

Thinking he was ready to head back to their suite, she let him pull her up. But instead of walking toward the hotel, he took her closer to the water's edge.

Moonlight splashed like silver across the surface of the water. The sky was filling rapidly with stars, scattered like fairy dust across the horizon.

How fanciful she was tonight. Wishes and fairy dust. It seemed appropriate for such a magical setting, though. Maybe she'd wake up in the morning and this would have all been a dream.

If that was the case, she was determined to exist in her dream world for as long as possible.

Without a word, Ryan took her in his arms and began to move to the distant strains of music. He gathered her close and she tucked her head beneath his chin, leaning into him as they swayed in time with the ocean and the soft melody lilting through the air.

Closer and closer they melted together until they were barely moving at all. She was tucked securely against his body, a perfect fit.

He laid his cheek atop her head and turned slowly, his feet guiding their rhythm.

Finally they stopped moving at all and stood locked together as night fell around them. He ran his fingers through her hair and kissed the top of her head.

She tilted back so that she looked into his eyes and she saw need and desire, but she also saw hope.

Her eyelids grew heavy as he slowly, ever so slowly, lowered his head until their mouths were so close but not yet touching. The moment stretched on, their breaths mingling, their gazes never breaking apart.

As the music drifted quietly away, he kissed her.

It was the most romantic, exquisite kiss she'd ever been given. It was a kiss that told her more than words ever could that this man cherished her. He wanted her. He would have her.

And when he finally pulled his mouth away, he tugged her into his arms and stood holding her tight as the moon bathed them in pale light.

Nine

Kelly pulled the nightgown over her head and warily glanced down her body. There was no doubt the garment was beautiful. A concoction of lace and satin that floated over her skin and molded to all the contours.

But she felt far too exposed. Her breasts looked too…big. Her belly looked enormous. Thank God she couldn't see her feet.

She eyed her door, knowing she was supposed to go to Ryan's room after she'd undressed for bed, but she couldn't seem to make herself take those few steps.

It wasn't that she didn't trust Ryan. No, it was

herself she didn't trust. She'd already made a big enough fool of herself when it came to this man. Once back in his arms, snuggled up close to him, she'd probably lose what little common sense she had left.

She sighed and sank onto the edge of her bed. Her hesitation was just another sad indication of the rift in their relationship. She'd never been inhibited around Ryan before.

He'd often be propped up in bed with his laptop, his brow creased in concentration as he worked on who knew what. She'd crawl into bed with exactly nothing on and tease and taunt him until his laptop and work were forgotten.

He used to laughingly say that he knew better than to bring work home because she never let him get away with it.

And now she couldn't even bring herself to walk into his bedroom.

A knock sounded at her door and then it opened a crack. Ryan stuck his head in. He stopped when he saw her sitting on the bed.

"Everything okay?"

She nodded.

He eased the door all the way open and walked in. He stood in front of her for a moment and then sat down on the bed next to her. He didn't say anything. He simply laid his hand on her lap, palm up, and waited for her to take it.

After a moment, she slid her hand over his. He twined his fingers through hers and squeezed gently. Then he stood and pulled her to her feet.

"We're both tired," he said. "Let's turn in and we'll worry about tomorrow when it gets here."

That didn't sound like the Ryan she knew. He was a man who planned everything to the nth degree. He had schedules, lists, planners, calendars. He not only worried about tomorrow, but the next year as well.

He led her into his bedroom and motioned for her to get into bed. He hung back, maybe out of deference to her obvious unease. Taking a deep breath, she crawled beneath the covers and turned so she'd face away from him when he got in.

The bed dipped behind her, and she felt his warmth as soon as he slid beneath the covers. He moved about for a few seconds and then the next thing she knew, he was flush against her back.

He wrapped one arm over her and pulled her in close. He nuzzled her hair before resting his cheek over her ear.

It was all she could do not to break down. It had been so long and it felt so right. Just like so many other nights in his arms. She'd missed him. Unbelievably, she'd missed him.

"No past," he murmured in her ear. "Just us. Right now."

She closed her eyes. It had been stupid to agree not to bring up the past. They might not talk about it but it loomed over them like a cloak of doom. It lay between them, awkward and unwieldy. There was no forgetting the past.

What they were doing was called denial. And it wasn't particularly effective.

He kissed her neck and snuggled a little closer. He cupped his hand over her belly affectionately. But the moment was bittersweet. This was how it should have been between them all along.

"Relax and go to sleep, Kell. I just want to hold you."

And oddly enough it was what she wanted too.

* * *

When Kelly opened her eyes, the first thing that registered was how comfortable she was. And warm. The second thing she realized was that she was on top of Ryan.

Not just on top of him, but sprawled across him as if she owned him. Her cheek was plastered to his shoulder and her forehead pressed against the side of his neck.

It was the way she'd woken every morning when they'd lived together.

Appalled that she could betray herself like this, she started to ease away but Ryan tightened his arm around her.

"Don't go. This is nice."

She raised her head and stared into eyes that were unclouded with sleep. Evidently he'd been awake for a while and content to lie there with her draped over him like a blanket.

"One thing hasn't changed," he said as he touched her cheek. "You're still beautiful when you wake up."

She soaked in the words, her heart tugging at the sincerity in his voice. Before she could question her sanity, she slowly lowered her mouth and touched it tentatively to his.

He seemed surprised and pleased by her taking the initiative. He lay still while she carefully explored his firm mouth.

She licked over the closed seam, and when his lips parted, she slid her tongue lightly over his bottom lip before moving inward to rasp over the end of his tongue.

Strong hands gripped her upper arms, holding her in place as he began to kiss her back. Softly at first, as if he was wooing her, and then harder. His breath sped up and came in little bursts through her mouth.

He sucked at the tip of her tongue and then she nipped at his when he let her go.

Before she realized it, she was on her back and he was over her, his knee between her legs as he devoured her mouth.

Hot. Breathless. Fast and hard and then slow and gentle.

With one hand he popped the two tiny buttons that held the bodice together. The material separated and her breasts strained precariously out of the gown. The satin caught on her hard, erect nipples and he tugged insistently until one breast came completely free.

He cupped the plump mound and then lowered his head, sucking the nipple into his mouth.

A shot of adrenaline slivered through her veins, edgy and sharp. She twisted restlessly beneath him as he sucked harder. She plunged her fingers through his short, cropped hair and then gripped the back of his head, holding him in place as she silently begged for more.

He pulled at her nipple, drawing his head back until the taut nub came free of his mouth. Then he lifted his gaze to meet hers and butterflies scuttled around her belly when she saw the look in his eyes.

"I want to make love to you, Kell. I need you so much. But I won't do this if it's only going to make things worse. You have to want this as much as I do."

"I want it more," she said hoarsely. And that was the truth. She'd always wanted him more. Craved him. Missed him when he wasn't with her.

Seeing him now, having him over her, his mouth on her, brought back those memories—happier memories—when things were perfect between them.

But had they been? Ever? Really?

She shook off the dark shadow that plagued her and reached up to caress his cheek.

"I need you, too."

Fire exploded in his eyes. Satisfaction and triumph glittered brightly as he swept down to claim her mouth again.

When he finally pulled back, he eased to the side and gathered her in his arms, holding her as if she was a precious piece of glass he was afraid might break.

For the longest time, his gaze stroked over her while he reacquainted himself with her all over again. Then he slid his hand over her shoulder and eased the strap of her gown down her arm.

He moved to the other side and hooked one finger in the strap, pulling it down until the gown bunched over the ball of her belly.

Levering up on one elbow, he coaxed her to lift her hips so he could pull the gown completely free. He worked it down her legs and then tossed it over the edge of the bed.

Now she was only clad in her underwear and it didn't feel like any sort of barrier to his gaze or his touch.

He cupped his hand just above her pelvis and caressed the round, firm bulge of her abdomen.

"Our baby," he said hoarsely.

Then he hovered over her and lowered his head so that his mouth pressed to the center of her belly in a tender kiss.

The gesture brought tears to her eyes, stinging the lids, and she swallowed against the quick knot that formed in her throat.

"Beautiful," he murmured. "I regret that I've missed watching her grow, watching you expand and watching your shape change. You're so unbelievably sexy."

"Her? You think it's a girl, too?"

Ryan smiled down at her. "You always say her. I guess I've just gotten used to it. I really don't care if it's a girl or boy. I just want you both to be okay."

She felt a little light-headed, as if she had an alcohol buzz without the alcohol.

He trailed his fingers lower, to her pelvis and through her damp, slick folds. She jumped in reaction when he brushed over her clitoris and then she moaned when he delved lower and carefully dipped the tip of his index finger inside her warmth.

"I love how you respond to me. I've always loved it."

She shifted restlessly as he continued his gentle exploration of her sensitive, quivering flesh. Already she was on edge, so close, and he'd only begun touching her.

She was impatient, wanting him now, but she also didn't want the sensation to end too quickly. After months without him, she wanted to savor every single moment with him.

"Spread your legs for me," he murmured.

Helpless to deny him, she relaxed her thighs and let them fall open as he moved down the bed. For a moment he got up and then he put his knee on the mattress, crawling between her thighs.

His eyes smoldered with heat and desire as he stared hungrily at her. Then he lowered himself, inserting one hand between her thighs to push them further apart.

She inhaled sharply and held her breath in anticipation as his head went down. He kissed her folds, right over her clitoris. Just a gentle, featherlike touch that had her spasming in need.

With careful fingers, he parted her flesh, exposing her to his mouth. He kissed her again, this time directly on the puckered, taut nub. Even as she arched, his tongue swept out and he licked from her opening to the top of the delicate hood that encased her most sensitive flesh.

She closed her eyes. Her fingers curled into tight balls, gathering the sheets and then releasing them once more as her body flew in about a dozen directions.

It was intense. It was wonderful. It was beautiful.

Something inside her shattered—or it felt like it. Wave after wave of sharp pleasure rolled over her with rigid intensity.

She panted softly, her breath squeezing from

lungs that felt robbed of air. Her hips lifted rhythmically off the mattress as he nuzzled her down from her orgasm.

When she gathered her senses and looked down, he was staring at her, satisfaction burning brightly in his blue eyes. There was a fierceness there that made her shiver, as if he was sending a silent message. *You're mine.*

With his hands cupped underneath her legs, he raised himself up. He pushed back enough that she was completely exposed to him and then reached between them to position himself at her opening.

She gasped at the hot, hard feel of him barely breaching her. And then he slid all the way in with one push.

It was enough to send her spiraling into another fast, reckless orgasm. She was still coming when he pulled back and pushed in again. Her body clutched desperately at him, hugging him tightly.

They both let out harsh sounds as he cupped her buttocks and lifted her so his angle put him even deeper.

"I can't hold on," he said. "It's too good. It's been too long. I'm sorry, baby."

She reached for him, clutching at his shoulders and pulling him to her. Still, he braced his hands on either side of her, holding his weight off her belly so that he didn't crush her.

He thrust, harder this time and she felt the shudder roll through his body as he held himself deep inside her.

He kissed her. Hungry. Passionate. With more desperation than she'd ever experienced from him. Their lovemaking had always been good, but he'd never lost control so quickly.

She kissed him with just as much hunger, her hands sliding down his back and then up again to hold his head to hers.

His hips trembled against her. They lay locked together, with him barely holding himself off her. Wanting that closeness to him—especially now—she urged him over to his side, rolling with him so they stayed together.

Their limbs were tangled, their arms wrapped tightly around each other, and he was still pulsing deep inside her body.

She tucked her head underneath his chin and breathed deeply of his scent, felt the erratic thump of his heart against her cheek.

It was easy to forget all that had happened between them. It was easy to forget the months of pain and loneliness. It was easy to imagine that they'd never been apart and that they were home in bed, just waking in Ryan's apartment—their apartment.

And just for a moment, she refused to allow the hazy euphoria to evaporate under the weight of reality.

Ten

Ryan lay there, Kelly in his arms, trying to sort out what had just happened. On the surface it had been a very quick, very hot sexual interlude. One of the best he'd ever had.

But it went deeper. It wasn't just sex. If it was just sex, his heart wouldn't feel as though it was going to burst out of his chest. He wouldn't be so overwhelmed that he had no idea how to process what he felt.

It was… It was more intense than sex had ever been between them. They had been a study in hot, flirty, fun in bed. He teased. She teased.

But this had been almost…heartbreaking, and

he couldn't shake the heaviness that pervaded his chest even now.

He rubbed his hand up and down her back and pressed a kiss to her hair in an effort to soothe some of the tightness in his throat.

He put a hand between them to touch her cheek and then he carefully pulled her away until he looked down into her eyes.

The stark emotion there. The devastation. It was like a knife to the gut. She looked so very vulnerable. Fragile. And scared. She looked scared to death.

Was she afraid of him? Of what had happened? He couldn't bear it if she hated herself for giving in to the overwhelming tension that had been building ever since he'd taken her back to New York.

"What are you thinking?" he asked hoarsely. "Tell me you don't regret this, Kell. Anything but regret."

Slowly she shook her head and he felt something loosen inside him. Relief. But it was only the first step.

He caressed her cheek, enjoying the feel of

her satiny skin. No matter how much he'd told himself that he was better off without her, that he was well rid of her, he could no longer lie to himself.

He wanted her. He wanted her back, no matter what she'd done in the past. He'd been forced to examine their relationship after he'd broken their engagement and ordered her out of his apartment—and his life. Maybe he'd been partially to blame. Maybe he'd worked too many hours. Maybe he'd neglected her.

Whatever the case, something had gone horribly wrong and he was determined to find the cause so that it didn't happen again.

Unable to resist, he kissed her forehead and then each eyelid. He gently kissed each cheekbone and then her mouth before nibbling a path to her ear.

Amazingly, his groin tightened and he swelled inside the clasp of her satiny flesh. He flexed his hips against her eliciting a low whimper as her fingers curled into his shoulder.

He slid easily in and out and he nudged her leg up with his own so that he had easier access.

"Do you like it here on your side?" he murmured. "Are you comfortable? Or would you prefer to be on top?"

She flushed and he smiled, delighted by this suddenly shy side of her. She'd never been bashful about taking the initiative in the past and suddenly he wanted to coax that out of her again.

Without waiting for her to respond, he gathered her in his arms and rolled so she was astride him, her hands planted on his chest for balance.

She was hot and tight around him and he clenched his teeth, closing his eyes as he sucked in steadying breaths. He'd already lost every ounce of control the first time. He wanted to make it last this time.

Her knees locked at his sides and she lifted her hips the tiniest bit before lowering her weight once more to surround him with silky, heated sweetness that had sweat beading his forehead.

She seemed inhibited and a little unsure and this new shyness from her continued to be endearing as hell. He reached for her, wanting to offer reassurance, but as his hands stroked up her lush body, over her swollen belly to her gorgeous breasts, he forgot all about offering her anything except the pleasure of his touch.

He stroked the swell of her breasts, enjoying the new fullness. Her nipples were darker, more pronounced, and his mouth watered with wanting to taste them again.

He pulled ever so gently at the tips, just enough to make them harden and pucker. She sucked in her breath and fluttered around his erection until he groaned and gritted his teeth to keep from orgasming.

"I love your body. You're beautiful pregnant, Kelly. I can't keep my hands or mouth off you. You make me crazy."

She smiled then, a brilliant smile that he felt all the way to his soul. Her eyes lit up and sparkled and he felt as if he'd been handed the world in the palm of her hand.

Hell, if that was all it took to make her smile like that, he'd gladly tell her every single day how gorgeous she was.

She reached for his hands, laced her fingers in his and then used his hands for leverage as she raised her hips just enough so he slid through her sweetness all over again.

His breath escaped in a long hiss and then she slid down, resheathing him all over again.

"You drive me crazy," he muttered.

She smiled, clearly satisfied with his admission.

He savored the feel of her much smaller hands engulfed by his. They held on tightly as she began a slow, rhythmic ride.

Their gazes locked. They never looked away, never broke eye contact as she made love to him, driving him closer and closer to ultimate release.

Her breaths grew more rapid and erratic. Her face became flushed and she tightened around him. She was close. He was closer. But he was determined to take care of her first.

It took every ounce of his concentration. His body strained. He was rigid, painfully rigid, and then she pulsed and went wet around him. Her body shuddered.

He pulled her down, holding her as he took control of their movements. He stroked and caressed her, kissing her hair, murmuring to her how beautiful she was.

As the last of her orgasm rolled through her body, his began. Through it all, their fingers remained entwined, their hands clasped.

He brought their hands to rest between them, against their chests, over their hearts, as he surged upward, his mind numb, his body awash with the sweetest of pleasure.

She collapsed over him, going limp as she nuzzled against his neck. She kissed him just below the ear and he smiled at the sweetness of the gesture.

He missed her affection. Missed the way she had always seemed to be touching him or kissing him or just offering him a smile.

He'd missed *her.*

And now he had to find a way to make sure she didn't leave again. He didn't think for a minute that sex was a fix-all for a relationship. It wasn't even a good bandage.

He knew it wasn't going to be easy. There was too much mistrust and hurt between them, but somehow they had to find their way back. He wouldn't allow himself to think any differently.

She was his. She carried his child. To him, that made things simple. She belonged with him. She needed him to take care of her. He wanted to take care of her.

If he was willing to forget the past, then shouldn't she be willing to try their relationship again? It wasn't as if he'd betrayed her.

But she carried so much hurt and anger. Something inside her had been broken. Had he done it when he'd tossed her out of his apartment? What had she expected?

He stroked her hair and willed himself not to become embroiled in the past. He'd promised himself—and her—that he'd put everything behind him.

And if he was willing to do that, then he saw no reason she shouldn't be willing to let the past rest as well.

"How about breakfast in bed?" he asked.

"Mmm, that sounds nice. I don't think I can move and I'm suddenly feeling lazy."

He smiled because he couldn't imagine anything better than the two of them sharing an intimate meal in bed. Hell, if he had his way they wouldn't leave the bedroom for the rest of the day.

"Let me go order room service. You stay here and get comfortable. I'll be right back."

He kissed her nose and then carefully disentangled himself from the warm clasp of her body. He eased her onto her side, pulled the rumpled sheet over her and rolled toward the nightstand, sitting up and putting his legs over the edge of the bed.

He glanced back to see that she'd immediately commandeered his pillow, which made him chuckle, because it was exactly what she'd done in the past.

He picked up the phone, ordered breakfast for them both and then rolled back over to face her.

"You can't have your pillow back," she mumbled.

He smiled and propped his head in his palm. "Never let it be said I interfered with the comfort of my woman."

One eyebrow went up and she studied him for

a long moment. He could see her mind swirling with something and so he simply waited to see if she'd say what was on her mind.

"Am I?" she finally asked.

His brow furrowed. "Are you what?"

"Yours," she said simply. "I need to know what this was, Ryan. Are we back together? I don't know what I'm supposed to do here and I'm not about to assume anything."

He took a deep breath because it was important to handle this just right. The last thing he wanted to do was screw everything up when he felt as if he was this close to having her where he wanted her.

"I think that's up to you," he said carefully. "I think I've been up front about what I want, about where I'd like to see our relationship. It's time for you to decide if this is where you want to be. With me. I'm not saying we have to take a huge leap, but we can at least decide to be together so we can work things out."

She visibly swallowed and he could see fear in her gaze again. It ate at his gut because he honestly didn't know what scared her so bad.

Was he such an ogre? Could she really blame him or hold against him the reaction he'd had to her being unfaithful?

"My mind tells me I'm an idiot for even considering this," she muttered.

"What does your heart tell you?" he asked softly.

She sighed and stared helplessly back at him, her blue eyes churning with emotion.

"My heart tells me that I want this. No matter how much I think I *shouldn't* want it, I do. Maybe this is a bad time to have a discussion about our relationship when our minds are mush after sex."

He touched his finger to her lips. "I think it's the perfect time to have it because our guards are down. It's just us. No barriers. No walls. Just us and how we feel."

"How *do* you feel, Ryan? Do you really want this?"

"Yeah, I do, Kell. I want it so damn much that the thought of you walking away has my gut in knots."

Her eyes widened. "But I never walked away from you."

He blew out his breath. “Let’s not talk about that, okay? Whatever happened in the past, the point is, I don’t want you to walk away *now.* I can’t stand the thought of it.”

“Okay,” she said so quietly he almost didn’t hear.

He reached out and nudged her chin up. “Okay?”

“I want to stay. I have no idea how we’ll work all this out, but I want to try.”

Satisfaction ripped through him, so savage that for a moment he couldn’t breathe. He had to temper his reaction because he wanted nothing more than to grab her, haul her into his arms and hold her so damn tight that she could never escape.

“We’ll do more than try,” he vowed. “We’re going to fix this, Kell. We’re going to make it work this time.”

Eleven

"She doesn't give up, does she?" Kelly murmured as she watched Roberta approach their table, a determined expression on her face.

Ryan looked up and to his credit heaved a sigh and appeared to be extremely irritated with the impending interruption. After a morning and most of the afternoon in bed, they'd ventured out for dinner and now here was Roberta, circling like a hawk.

And it wasn't that Kelly was jealous. Honestly, Roberta wasn't Ryan's type, though she supposed his type could have changed after he'd broken their engagement.

What bothered her was the seemingly public knowledge of their relationship. It just proved Kelly's assertion that his family and friends alike loathed her. Something Ryan was finally coming to accept. But acceptance didn't make anything easier.

While love was supposed to be "everything," she wasn't naive enough to think that relatives hating you didn't put an unbearable strain on a relationship. Who could be happy when, at every turn, your lover's family did everything they could to make their disapproval known?

Maybe they'd both been too naive the first time. Maybe now they could be stronger together. But then what would happen if and when Ryan finally knew the truth about Jarrod? And his mother's part in the whole affair?

Once again, Kelly would be the wedge between him and his family. Their relationship might not survive a second time.

Roberta stopped at the table and bent to kiss Ryan on either cheek, but when he turned away, she caught him full on the lips, leaving a smear of lipstick.

Kelly sighed and sat back, resigned to another uncomfortable scene.

Ryan looked…pissed.

"Roberta, what the hell?"

He didn't even try to be polite this time.

"Oh, I just came around to say goodbye. My flight leaves in the morning and I hoped we could set up a time to get together when you return to New York. Your mother would like us all to have dinner."

She flicked a sideways look of disdain—and challenge—in Kelly's direction, but Kelly purposely yawned and sent a bored look in return.

Roberta frowned but turned eagerly back to Ryan. "Shall we say this weekend perhaps? I'm sure Kelly wouldn't mind. After all, you and I are old friends."

"I mind," Ryan said in a clipped voice. "Now if that's all, we'd appreciate being left to our meal."

"I'll call you," Roberta murmured. "We'll talk…later." The inference being they'd talk when Kelly wasn't around. Was the woman stupid?

It was tempting to put her firmly in her place,

but frankly it would take too much effort and Kelly was quite content to remain in her seat and watch Roberta stew in her own ignorance.

Roberta touched Ryan's face in a gesture that repulsed Kelly then slid one long nail down his jaw before fluttering her fingers at him as she walked away.

Ryan turned, his lips tight. "God, I'm sorry, Kell. You have to know I haven't encouraged her."

Kelly smiled and handed him a napkin to wipe the lipstick off his mouth. "Yeah, I figured that much out. She's…she's interesting. And awfully dense. You were pretty blatant with the brush-off. It makes me wonder what your mother promised her."

Ryan frowned as he swiped at his lips. He pulled the napkin away, frowning even harder at the red smear on the material. Then he reached across the table and took her hand. "Let's not let her ruin what has otherwise been a spectacular day."

Kelly rolled her eyes. "You're just saying that because of the sex. Give a man sex and it's the most amazing day ever."

He grinned. "Well, there is that, but it's not just sex with you, Kell. It's…more."

She flushed in pleasure at the sincerity in his voice. He made her believe all sorts of crazy things, like they could actually work through the serious issues facing them.

"So what do you want to do after dinner?" she asked lightly.

"How about another walk on the beach? Maybe we'll stop in the cabana down the way for some dancing."

"I liked how we danced last night," she said in a dreamy voice. "Just you and me. No one else around. It was an amazing night."

He studied her for a long moment, his fingers idly caressing hers. "Yeah, it was." He lifted her hand and brought it to his mouth where he proceeded to kiss each fingertip before turning her hand over and nuzzling into her palm. "I thought maybe tomorrow we could get out and see some of the sights as long as you're feeling up to it. I don't want you walking, but I've arranged for a convertible so we can drive where we like. Top down, wind-in-our-hair sort of thing."

"It sounds fun." And it had been a long time since she'd simply had fun. She smiled, feeling her chest grow lighter with each passing second. Impulsively she squeezed his hand.

"I love that you're smiling again," he said. "You're beautiful when you smile. I want you to be happy, Kell. I'll do whatever it takes to make you happy."

With that statement, she felt some of her hurt and anger recede. For the first time she began to believe that maybe they could get beyond the past and forge ahead.

He seemed so sincere. Whatever he thought of her in the past, he seemed willing to push aside those feelings and start over. Why would he go to such lengths if he didn't care about her?

"I want this to work," she said earnestly. And for the first time she really believed wholeheartedly that she did. That they could find their way back to each other seemed an impossible dream. It would take forgiveness and sacrifice, but she wanted it more than anything.

* * *

"Let me see your feet," Ryan said as he lowered himself onto the couch next to her.

He reached down, took her feet and maneuvered them until they rested on his lap. He examined them with the precision of a physician, testing for swelling. Then he settled into a gentle massage until she all but wilted in pleasure.

"They're looking better. The swelling's down quite a bit." He paused for a moment, his hands still moving over her arches, and stared at her. "You look better, Kell."

"Thanks. I think," she said in amusement.

His expression grew serious. "You looked tired and worn down when I found you in Houston."

"I was," she admitted. "But I'd rather not talk about it."

"Yet another thing that's off-limits?"

She shrugged. "Nothing good can come of it."

"I worried I kept you on your feet too much this evening," he said as he continued to rub. "But I enjoyed dancing with you on the beach. It was an excuse to hold you."

She smiled and leaned back, allowing the pleasure of his touch to wash through her body. "I feel fine. Really. Not so tired anymore. I have more energy now than I've had since early in my pregnancy. Being on my feet all the time eventually wore me down."

He went silent and he looked brooding, his expression intense. He massaged her soles and then worked up to her toes.

He seemed to battle whether or not he wanted to speak, but finally he locked his gaze with hers and said, "Why didn't you cash the check, Kelly? I gave it to you so you'd be provided for. No matter what you did, how angry I was or how things were between us, I intended you to be cared for. Do you have any idea what it did to me to find you working in that god-awful place and living in a dive, barely making it? Hell, you didn't even have food in your apartment."

"I ate at the diner," she said.

He made a sound of exasperation. "Like that's supposed to make me feel any better? Why didn't you use the money? You could have finished college. You could have lived for a long time to come without ever having to work."

"I have pride. It took a beating but it's still intact. I guess if I hadn't been able to find a job and the choice was between starving or taking money that made me feel dirty, I would have sucked it up and done it anyway."

"Did you hate me so much?" he asked hoarsely. "That you would rather work in such deplorable conditions than accept anything from me?"

She leveled a stare at him. "Don't ask questions you aren't prepared to hear the answers to."

He closed his eyes. "That's answer enough, I suppose."

She shrugged. "You hated me, too."

He shook his head and her eyes widened. "No? Ryan, you said and did some terrible things. Not the least of which was tossing that check at me with so much disdain that I can still remember the way I felt."

"What did you expect?" he asked. "For God's sake, Kelly, I'd just found out you slept with my brother. You had my ring on your finger, we were planning our wedding and you slept with my *brother.*"

"And of course he's blameless in the whole

thing," she said scornfully. "Tell me, Ryan, how long did it take you to forgive him? How long before he was coming back over and you were having family dinners at your mother's?"

His face flushed a dull red and then he dragged a hand raggedly through his hair. "It took a while, all right? I was furious with him—and you. I had to decide whether to allow what happened to ruin our relationship. He's family. He's my brother."

She leaned forward, forgetting their vow not to dredge up the past. "And I was the woman you were supposed to marry, Ryan. Didn't I deserve anything from you? Besides a payoff and a get-the-hell-out-of-my-life?"

"I'm here now," he said quietly. "I was angry. I had a right to be. I won't apologize for that. But I'm here now and I want us to try again. We both made mistakes."

She had to let go of the resentment and anger that still bubbled up every time they spoke of the past. She had to put it away because there was no way for her to win.

She leaned back again and wiggled her foot in his hand to hint for him to continue his massage.

"So where are we going to drive tomorrow? Should I wear one of those scarves and huge sunglasses so I look chic?"

He relaxed, relief stark in his eyes that she was letting the matter drop.

"Wear that very sexy sundress that Jansen bought you."

She arched an eyebrow. "Which one? He bought several."

"Clearly you haven't seen the one then. Or you'd know what I was talking about. It's red. Perfect with your coloring. Strapless, clingy in all the right places. Just make sure to bring something to protect your head from the sun."

"It sounds fun. Carefree," she said wistfully. It had been far too long since she'd done anything remotely resembling carefree.

"I intend for us to have a lot of fun together again, Kell. We used to. We were happy."

She had to acknowledge that they had been. Once. So she nodded and he smiled.

"Are you ready for bed yet?" he asked.

"Depends on what you have in mind," she murmured.

A gleam entered his eyes and he slid his hands up her legs, stroking and caressing.

"Well, I sure wasn't planning to go to sleep. Not for a good long while."

"In that case, definitely take me to bed."

He rose and then unexpectedly he reached down, slid his arms beneath her and lifted her up, cradling her against his chest.

"Ryan, put me down. I'm too heavy!"

He silenced her with a kiss. "A—you're still a little bit of a thing. And B—are you suggesting I'm not manly enough to carry my woman around?"

She laughed. "Forget I said anything. Carry on then."

Twelve

There weren't enough words to explain how much she dreaded getting on that plane and flying back to New York. The past two days had had a dreamlike quality. They were like the best fantasy imaginable, unmarred by a single incident.

And now they were going back to reality.

Cold, gloomy New York City.

She hadn't always felt that way about the city but now it only held bad memories for her. She wasn't as optimistic as Ryan that they could somehow pull the pieces of their relationship back together and sustain it with so many factors against them.

As if sensing her reluctance, Ryan slid an arm around her waist and urged her onto the plane.

A few moments later, they were seated and Ryan reached over to buckle her seat belt for her.

"It's going to be all right, Kell. Trust me."

She wished it was that easy.

Still, she offered him a reassuring smile and settled back for the flight.

But it was Ryan who seemed to grow more tense as the flight neared its end. He touched her frequently, and at first she thought it was to ease her nerves, but she wondered now if it was to reassure himself.

Did he think she'd bolt and run as soon as they landed? She might be tempted but she'd given him her promise and she intended to keep it. Even if it killed her.

They hadn't really talked about what would happen when they got back to New York. Maybe they'd both been too determined not to ruin their time on the island.

Once again when they landed, there was a car waiting for them, and Ryan hurried her out of the cold and into the warm confines of the vehicle.

A mixture of snow and sleet fell from gray skies and she shivered even though the heat was on full blast in the back of the car. It was a shock to leave sunshine and sandy beaches for the bitter chill of New York in the throes of a cold front.

The euphoria that had enveloped much of their stay on the island evaporated and depression settled over her until her mood matched the weather.

Ryan pulled her into his side and kissed her temple. "I have a distinct urge to order in tonight, eat in front of the fire and then make love to you for the rest of the night."

She sighed and snuggled into his side. Somehow he'd known just what to say to make some of the oppressive worry melt away.

"I had fun with you the last few days," she said, wanting him to have that admission at least.

"I'm glad. I had fun with you too. It felt like old times, only…better."

She nodded because it had been better. More honest. Or maybe they hadn't taken a single moment for granted as they'd done in the past.

They'd enjoyed every single minute together, making the most of each one.

They'd laughed and loved and they'd made love. The very last day they hadn't left their hotel room. Their meals had been delivered and they'd stayed in bed, only leaving it to take a leisurely shower together.

She wished it could have lasted.

But they had to face the music sooner or later.

"I had Jansen make you an appointment to see the doctor tomorrow. I want to be sure everything is okay with you and the baby."

She smiled, loving the concern in his voice. "Spending the time away with you did more for me than any doctor ever could."

He looked pleased with her response, pleased that she'd admitted it. He bent to kiss her again as they pulled up outside Ryan's apartment building.

Ryan hastily got out, helped Kelly from the car and rushed her out of the cold and into the building. As they rode up in the elevator, Kelly realized just how much she dreaded being back here, in this apartment. In this city.

"My driver will bring the luggage up soon. Why don't you go get comfortable on the couch? I'll turn the fire on and fix us something to drink. Are you hungry?"

"Hmm, no, but I'd love Thai takeout later. For now I'll have some juice."

"Thai sounds good. Get comfortable. Take your shoes off and prop your feet up. I bet your ankles are swelling from sitting with your feet down for that long."

Kelly chuckled at the mother hen sound to his voice but did as he said and settled on the sumptuous leather couch. She kicked off her shoes and winced at the puffy look of her ankles as she propped them on the ottoman.

She'd have the doctor and Ryan both griping at her, but heck, she'd done nothing except eat good food, rest and relax for the past several days. What more could she do?

Ryan had just set their drinks on the coffee table and settled next to her when his phone started ringing. She supposed it was to be expected since he'd been out of the country. It wasn't as if his being tied up with work was anything new. In the past, though, she'd never hesitated to needle him or distract him. Something that had both exasperated and thrilled him in equal parts.

But now she sat quietly as he fished his BlackBerry out of his pocket.

His lips thinned a bit before he put the phone to his ear.

"Hello, Mom."

Kelly sighed. That hadn't taken long.

Ryan wasn't one of those guys who was tied to the apron strings, but he respected his mother, as any son should, and like most children, she supposed, had a bit of a blind spot when it came to her.

Or maybe he just didn't want to see her as the conniving vindictive witch that Kelly knew her to be. Kelly was sure his mother had her good points. She obviously loved her sons. But she'd never be someone Kelly would warm to. Ever.

"Yes, we're back. Listen, Mom, why did you send Roberta there? I don't appreciate you interfering. I won't tolerate any disrespect toward Kelly. You need to accept that she's with me. If you can't do that, then you and I are going to have a serious problem."

Kelly's eyes rounded. There was anger in Ryan's voice and his eyes were hard.

"We'll see," he continued. "Right now Kelly and I need some time together without interference, no matter how well meaning. I'll call you when we're ready to have dinner together."

Ugh. It took all of Kelly's control not to make a face. But this was Ryan's mother. This was her child's grandmother, no matter how much Kelly wished it to be different.

"I love you too, Mom. Let me go. We just got in and we're both tired."

He tossed the BlackBerry on the couch. Kelly looked inquisitively at him.

"Mom wants to express her apologies for Roberta's actions. And her own. She wants to have dinner with us one night. I told her I'd be in touch when we were ready for that."

There wasn't anything she could say so she remained silent. She leaned forward to pick up her glass of orange juice to mask the awkwardness of the moment and leaned back, sipping at the sweet and tart drink.

He glanced at her propped-up feet and then frowned. "Your feet are pretty swollen."

She lifted one and sighed. "Yeah. Apparently I'm a water-retaining cow."

"Are they hurting? Want me to rub them?"

"No, I'm fine. They ache a little but right now I don't want anyone touching them. I'll just sit like this for the rest of the evening and drink lots of water. The potassium in the OJ will help."

He leaned over and kissed her forehead just as the buzzer sounded.

"That'll be our luggage. Be right back."

She adjusted her position so that some of the tension was relieved in her back. The truth was she was tired of sitting after being on the airplane for so many hours, but neither did she want to be on her feet with swollen and aching ankles.

Deciding to dispense with sitting at all, she turned on her side, stuck a cushion between her legs and let out a sigh at the bliss of being off her behind and her feet.

She stared across the room out the panels of

glass that led onto the balcony and watched as a few snowflakes spiraled downward. The weather didn't seem to be able to make up its mind whether it wanted to rain, sleet or snow; but, at least for now, a few fat flakes were falling.

The flames from the gas fireplace gave the living room a warm, homey feel and as she adjusted her gaze to the fireplace, lethargy stole over her.

She reached for the throw draped on the back of the couch and pulled it over her body, sighing that she finally felt comfortable after traveling for so long.

Her eyelids were drooping and she didn't fight the urge to sleep. Ryan would wake her in time for dinner.

When Ryan returned to the living room, he found Kelly fast asleep on the couch, her hand tucked under her cheek. He was struck by how young and innocent she looked. Not at all like someone who played brother against brother.

He supposed it was unfair to think such

thoughts when they'd both made an effort to get beyond the past, but the dark thoughts always crept in.

What fault did he have that would cause Kelly to seek comfort with his brother? And why had she been vengeful enough to want to ruin his relationship with his only sibling when Jarrod had told her that he was going to confess to Ryan that they'd had sex?

Ryan felt more like a father to Jarrod than a brother. Eight years separated them in age and their father had died when Ryan was barely a teenager. He'd stepped in, assuming the paternal role with Jarrod, who was still a boy.

He'd attended all his baseball games, taken him to sporting events. Taken him to movies. He'd been there for his graduation from high school. Had helped him move when he went off to college and supported his decision to return home and pursue a career in finance.

Nothing should come between brothers. Certainly not a woman. But one had. Kelly had. Not only had it struck a blow to his relationship with Jarrod that he still hadn't recovered from but it had destroyed his relationship with Kelly as well.

A relationship he was determined to rebuild.

But to go forward, he had to determine what had gone wrong in the past.

No matter what they'd vowed, at some point the past had to be addressed. It couldn't be ignored forever.

He picked up his phone and quietly walked into the next room to call Devon and Cam.

Thirteen

Ryan took Kelly to the doctor the next day. She'd assumed that *she* would go to the doctor. As in alone. And that Ryan would go back to work since he'd been out of the office for nearly a week.

But he'd ridden with her, gone into the exam room with her and stuck to her side throughout the entire appointment.

The doctor made noises about the swelling and noted that there was still protein in her urine. He asked her endless questions about how she felt and then issued a stern lecture about taking it easy.

Ryan latched on to every word and by the time they left, Kelly was sure that he'd lock her in her bedroom and not allow her out until the baby was born.

She was prepared to be stir-crazy in advance, but he said nothing. When they arrived back at the apartment, he didn't make her prop her feet up even though that was precisely what she did as soon as they walked through the door.

"I think as long as you don't overdue it that there's no reason you can't get around in moderation," Ryan said. "The doctor was in agreement that we just need to watch you closely for any change and be sensitive to when you're not feeling well to make sure it doesn't develop into something more serious."

Thank God he was prepared to be reasonable.

"I thought we could eat out tonight if you feel up to it. It's cold but it's not supposed to snow or sleet. I know you like going out."

Touched that he'd remembered—although she wasn't sure why he wouldn't—she smiled and nodded in excitement. She did love the city at night. Loved the lights, the cozy restaurants and little hole-in-the-wall cafés and local eateries.

"I sent Jansen out for warmer clothing and a coat for you. Just until you feel up to shopping for yourself," he said. "I'll go with you when you want to. Just say the word."

Knowing how much Ryan hated shopping, she was touched and idiotically emotional over the fact that he'd offered to go with her.

"We should also think about going shopping for the baby very soon," Ryan said in a husky voice.

She blinked in surprise. But then she stared down at her belly and realized that he was right. She only had a short time—weeks—until the baby would arrive. Six weeks? But babies often came early. And she was horribly unprepared.

In Houston she'd lived from paycheck to paycheck, just praying to be able to make rent and save money for when she had to take time off when the baby was born. There hadn't been money for all the things people bought in preparation for a baby, so she'd never even thought about it.

Panicked now that she realized how unprepared she was, she stared in dismay at Ryan.

"Hey," he said as he scooted over next to her. "I didn't mean to stress you out. I thought you'd be excited to shop for the baby."

"I don't have anything," she confessed. "No baby clothing. No crib. Diapers. Oh God, I don't even know what-all I need. I was always happy to just make it through another day in Houston. I never looked ahead. It was too overwhelming."

He gathered her in his arms and held her as he ran his hand soothingly over her hair. "There's no hurry, okay? I'll send out for some parenting books and magazines and for the next few days, I want you to rest, put your feet up and do as much reading as you like. Make a list. We'll look at stuff together. It'll be fun. We still have plenty of time before she gets here."

She squeezed him in a tight hug. "Thank you. I think you just prevented a meltdown. I feel so awful. I don't even have any cute baby booties. What kind of mother am I going to be?" she asked mournfully.

He squeezed her back. "You'll be a wonderful

mom. You've had a lot to deal with. Cut yourself some slack, okay? Now why don't you go take a long soaking bath and get ready for dinner?"

She reached up and pulled him down to kiss him. It was on the tip of her tongue to say she loved him, but she swallowed the words and kissed him again instead.

He kissed her back, lingering over her lips, savoring the taste and feel of her.

It shouldn't make her feel so sad that she still loved him. But she couldn't shake the heaviness from her chest as she pulled away and then got up and headed for the bathroom.

"I got a call from Rafael today," Ryan said over dinner.

Kelly frowned. "How is he doing? I still can't believe he got into a plane crash, lost his memory and then fell in love with a woman he completely screwed over for land."

Ryan winced. "You make it sound so..."

She lifted an eyebrow. "Awful? I know he's your friend, but he's always been arrogant and a bit of a jerk. Especially toward women. He never liked me."

"Rafe has changed. I know it sounds weird, but after his accident he did a one-eighty. Anyway, he and Bryony are back from their honeymoon and they're coming into town in a few days to put his apartment on the market."

"He's moving?"

That shocked Kelly. Rafael was an urbanite through and through. He loved the city. Loved to travel. She couldn't imagine him anywhere else.

"Yeah, he and Bryony are going to maintain a residence on Moon Island."

"Wow. Rafael must really be in love."

"Amazing what men in love will do for the women they love," Ryan said softly.

Kelly didn't meet his gaze and concentrated instead on her soup. Lobster bisque. After six months of bland diner food, she savored every bite. Her taste buds were all simultaneously orgasming.

She'd eaten more in the past week than she had in all those months in Houston, and she was going to balloon like a blowfish if she kept this up. She'd even closed her eyes when they'd weighed her at her doctor's appointment the previous day, not wanting to know how much weight she'd gained.

"He wants us all to get together."

Her eyes narrowed. "Define us."

"Me, you, Dev and Cam and, of course, Rafael and Bryony. I also thought it would be good to invite Mom so you'd have the buffer of other people. We can get it over with in one clean sweep."

It sounded like an evening from hell, not that she'd admit that to him. She couldn't imagine anything worse than being surrounded by Ryan's closest friends, who of course all had been told that she'd cheated on Ryan with Jarrod. She nearly bared her teeth in response to that thought. And then there was his darling mother. All the evening lacked was…Jarrod.

"And Jarrod?" she asked icily.

"He won't be invited. I wouldn't do that to you, Kell," Ryan said quietly.

"When is this supposed to take place?"

"Next week. Probably at the end of the week. They'll be busy organizing his apartment. We'll eat at Tony's. You like it there. It's nice and casual. We can leave at any time and there won't be any obligation to stay and visit."

She sighed. She had to hand it to him. He was working hard to make things as easy for her as possible. The least she could do is be accommodating. His friends were important to him. His mother was important to him.

"All right," she said in a low voice. "Of course we can go." She forced a smile. "It'll be nice to see everyone again." She nearly choked on the lie, but the relief in Ryan's eyes made it worth it.

He reached for her hands. "We're going to make it this time, Kell."

She caught his fingers and returned his squeeze. "It makes me feel better to know you think so."

"Do you have doubts?"

"I'd be lying if I said I didn't. I'm scared witless. I'm scared to go out of your apartment," she said honestly. "I don't like the person I've become, but it doesn't change the fact that I'm a very different person than the Kelly you knew. I'm more cautious now. I'm…harder. I don't like it about myself, but I've learned to be that way out of necessity."

He took her hand in both of his and propped his elbows on the table as he stared over at her.

"Marry me."

She jerked her hand back in shock and stared at him. *"What?"* Where the hell had that come from?

"Marry me."

He withdrew one hand and then reached into his pocket to pull out a small ring box. With his thumb, he flipped it open and she saw a stunning diamond ring nestled in velvet.

He held it out to her and she lifted her gaze to stare at him as if he'd lost his mind.

"I couldn't decide whether or not to give you back your old one or buy you a new one. I kept the old ring. I kept it with me the entire time you were gone. But then I decided that we deserve a fresh start. So I bought a new one for a new beginning."

Her hand trembled in his and she stared speechlessly at him.

He ruefully shook his head. “I know it’s not the most romantic proposal. It’s not even under the best circumstances. I’d intended to wait. Until it was the right time. Until we’d sorted out things between us. But I couldn’t wait any longer. And when my friends and family see you again, I want them to know that we’re together, that you’re the woman I’m going to marry and that you have my support.”

Tears filled her eyes and her chest ached with emotion. He made no move to take the ring out of the box and put it on her finger for her. He simply held it in the palm of his hand, waiting for her to make the decision.

“But Ryan,” she began helplessly. “There’s so much… The past…”

“Shh,” he murmured. “I know what you’re saying. We have a lot to talk about. We have a lot to work out. But I wanted to do this first so that you know that no matter what comes out when we eventually revisit the past that I still want to marry you. I need you to know that. Maybe it’ll help. Maybe it'll make it easier knowing that it won't change things between us *now.*"

She wiped furiously at the moisture on her cheeks, determined not to ruin the moment by breaking down. "In that case, yes. I'll marry you."

He looked thunderstruck, like maybe he really hadn't expected her to agree. And then he smiled and such joy flashed across his face that it left her breathless. His eyes lit up and his grip on her hand tightened until her fingertips were bloodless.

He fumbled with the box, took the ring out. The hand he held hers with shook as he positioned her finger so he could slide the ring on.

Then he leaned across the table and kissed her. When he pulled away, he still held her hand and he suddenly stood, pulling her to her feet.

"Let's go," he said hoarsely. "Let's go home where we can be alone. I just want to hold you away from everyone else."

She went willingly into his arms and they walked past the other diners, uncaring of the stares they received. She never felt the cold, brisk air as they exited the restaurant and walked to the curb where Ryan's car waited.

For once she felt warm on the inside. After feeling cold and alone for so long, sunshine rushed through her veins.

Fourteen

Kelly woke to find Ryan gone from bed. She rolled to check the clock on the nightstand and realized why she was alone. It was after nine and Ryan would have long since gone into the office.

When they'd returned from St. Angelo, Kelly had moved into Ryan's room. It wasn't as though a big production had been made. He'd simply carried her luggage into his room. And when it was time for bed, he'd carried her to his bed.

And she'd stayed.

How easily they'd fallen back into a comfortable routine. Just like before.

Before, it had been easy to take for granted the

rapport between them. The comfort and trust. She hadn't known then as she knew now how quickly things could be broken.

Even now she questioned how it could have happened.

There was always an excuse, a reason. He hadn't loved her enough. He hadn't trusted her. Their relationship was too new to weather something so difficult.

But no matter the reason, the end result had been the same. When things had gotten difficult, their relationship had crumbled like stale bread.

It didn't speak well for their future.

But she wouldn't think of that right now. Sure, it was stupid of her to allow herself to have such faith in him. But hope was a powerful thing. It made a person willingly blind to the truth.

She kept telling herself maybe this time…

Maybe this time they would truly get things right. Even if it meant forever bearing the burden of having the man she loved think she'd betrayed him with another man. His brother.

So many times she wanted to confront him. She wanted to try again to make him listen to her. Make him hear the truth. But each time she bit her lip because what purpose would it serve?

He might not believe her. He might. But would it change anything in the past? Would it change their future?

It wouldn't even make her feel any better because she knew the truth. Ryan believed she'd lied to him but he wanted to forget and move on. Was she an idiot to want more than that? Was she stupid to want him to know how wrong he'd been?

It was a dilemma that plagued her every single day that she and Ryan were back together. Part of her wanted to make him listen and to demand that he accept that he'd been wrong if he expected her to give this whole thing another shot.

Another part of her told her that her pride and her anger were barriers to her own happiness.

Wasn't a life with Ryan what she ultimately wanted? Did it matter how she achieved that goal?

She stared up at the ceiling as she lay in bed.

Yeah, it did. It really did. She couldn't go through their life together knowing it was in the back of Ryan's mind that she'd slept with someone else when she'd promised to be faithful to him.

She had to accept that what she really feared was that when she did confront Ryan, he'd reject her all over again, and if that happened, she knew she couldn't spend her life with someone who didn't trust her.

She was a coward, but it was the cold, hard truth that fear was what held her back. Not pride. Not anything else. She knew that if he didn't believe her this time they could never be together.

Not wanting the weight of anxiety to bear down on her today, she shook the bleak thoughts from her mind and crawled out of bed. She padded into the living room to see that Ryan had turned the fire on for her.

To her further surprise, she found a breakfast tray waiting for her on the table with bagels, cheese and an assortment of fruit.

But what caught her eye was the tiny pair of yellow baby booties.

She picked up the soft, fuzzy little booties, her throat knotting as she read the accompanying card.

Because you said you didn't have a pair yet. Love, Ryan.

She sank into the seat, her eyes stinging with tears. She held the booties to her cheek and then touched the card, tracing the scrawl of his signature.

"I shouldn't love you this much," she whispered. God, but she couldn't help herself. She craved him. He was her other half. She didn't feel whole without him.

And so began a courting ritual that tugged on her heartstrings.

Every morning when she crawled out of bed, there was a new present waiting for her from Ryan.

There was a baby book that outlined everything she could expect from birth through the first year of life. One morning he left her two outfits. One for a boy and one for a girl. *Just in case,* he had written.

On the fifth morning, he simply left her a

note that told her a gift was waiting in the extra bedroom.

Excited, she hurried toward the bedroom she'd once occupied and threw open the door to see not one present but a room full of baby things.

A stroller. A crib that was already put together. A little bouncy thing. An assortment of toys. A changing table. She couldn't take in all the stuff that was there. She didn't even know what all of it was for.

How on earth had he managed to sneak this in without her hearing?

And there by the window was a rocking chair with a yellow afghan lying over the arm. She walked over and reverently touched the wood, giving the chair an experimental push.

It creaked once and then swayed gently back and forth.

Already her feet protested her being up, so she moved the blanket and sat, staring around at the room full of treasures for their child.

She had been more tired in the past couple of days, but she'd been careful not to worry Ryan.

He'd worked so hard to make each day special for her.

If possible, she had fallen more deeply in love with him than ever before.

Tonight was the dinner with his friends and his mother, but even that couldn't dim her excitement or her happiness. And maybe that had been his plan all along. To take extra measures to make sure she knew that he supported her against any possible animosity or disdain.

It had certainly worked, because she couldn't imagine anything they could do or say that would make the cloud she walked on evaporate.

Ryan cared about her. He wanted to marry her. What else mattered?

She hugged that thought to her later as she picked through her clothing, trying to find the perfect outfit to wear to the dinner.

Before, it wouldn't even occur to her that an outfit was too sexy or revealing. If it looked good on her, and if she knew Ryan would like it, that was her only criteria.

But now she worried that with the sentiment already being that she was a…slut…she would merely perpetuate that belief if she wore anything that wasn't ultraconservative. And that pissed her off. She shouldn't care what these people thought of her. But it wasn't that easy. They were important to Ryan and Ryan was important to her.

Warm hands suddenly stole over her body, sliding around to her belly. She was drawn into a hard chest and sensual lips nibbled at her neck.

She sighed and relaxed into Ryan, her pulse speeding up.

"Is there a particular reason you're standing in your closet staring at your clothes?" he murmured against her ear.

She turned and laced her arms around his neck as she rose up on tiptoe to kiss him. "You're home early."

"Couldn't wait to see you. So what's with the closet?"

Her lips twisted into a frown and she let out a disgruntled sigh. "Just trying to find something to wear tonight. Something that doesn't make me look like the tramp they think I am."

Ryan's expression gentled and he trailed a

finger over her cheekbone. Taking her arms, he backed out of her closet and toward the bed until the back of his legs bumped against the mattress.

He sat down and pulled her down with him.

"You'll look beautiful no matter what you wear. Stop worrying so much."

"I know. It's silly. I can't help it. I'm nervous."

"I don't want you to worry, Kell. The past is in the past. I don't know that I've ever said the words, but I forgive you. And if I can forgive you then they should be able to do the same."

She went completely still. Pain jolted through her chest as if someone had stabbed her. Not that she knew what it felt like but it couldn't be worse than this.

He forgave her.

For something she'd never done. For something he refused to believe she hadn't done.

It took all the strength she possessed not to react, not to lash out. He hadn't said it to hurt her. but he couldn't possibly imagine how much she was bleeding inside right now.

He was trying to do the generous thing. He was trying to make her feel at ease.

He kissed her gently on the brow. "We both made mistakes. I'm not blameless. The important thing is that we never let what happened in the past happen again."

Numbly she nodded. She didn't trust herself to speak. What could she say?

She closed her eyes and leaned into him. He hugged her to him and rubbed his hand up and down her back. He offered comfort. He thought she was worked up about tonight. How could he possibly know that his "forgiveness" made her want to die?

He eased her to the side until she was perched on the edge of the bed and then he stood and walked into the closet. After a moment, he returned with a gorgeous, midnight-blue dress. He held it up and smiled.

"This one would look fantastic on you."

She struggled to collect her shattered senses and pretend that nothing was wrong.

"It's awfully…clingy," she said. "I'd look eleven months' pregnant in it."

"I love your belly," he said in an ultrasexy voice that sent shivers down her spine. "I love that this shows the world you're pregnant with my baby. You'll look gorgeous. Wear it for me."

There wasn't a woman alive who could refuse a request like that. She nodded silently, her heart aching all the while.

He laid the dress carefully on the bed and then bent down to kiss her once more.

"I'll leave you to get ready. The driver will be here for us in an hour."

She clung to him a little longer than was necessary but he didn't seem to mind. He touched her cheek as he pulled away and then walked toward the bathroom, loosening his tie as he went.

She stared at the dress. It was a fabulous creation. And it would definitely highlight her pregnancy, something Ryan seemed very keen on.

She closed her eyes. He forgave her. She wanted to weep.

It should be her who had to offer forgiveness. Not him.

Fifteen

Kelly swallowed her mounting dread as she and Ryan entered the restaurant. Ryan spoke in low tones to the maître d' and then they were ushered to a table in the back.

Ryan broke into a broad smile when he saw Rafael already seated next to a woman Kelly assumed was his wife, Bryony. Ryan's mother was also seated, as were Devon and Cameron. Just great. They were last to arrive, and so they made an "entrance."

Kelly stood by Ryan's side as he greeted everyone, then said, "Of course, you all remember Kelly. Except for you, Bryony."

He turned to Kelly. “Kelly, this is Bryony de Luca, Rafael’s wife. Bryony, this is my fiancée, Kelly Christian.”

The room went absolutely silent at his declaration. The expressions ranged from his mother’s ill-disguised horror to outright disbelief on his friends’ faces.

Even Bryony looked skeptical as she rose to extend her hand to Kelly. It was then that Kelly noticed that Bryony appeared every bit as pregnant as Kelly was.

“It’s nice to meet you,” Bryony said with what looked to be a forced smile.

Hell, how much could Bryony possibly know about Kelly anyway? It wasn’t as if she’d been around for that long. But she, like the others, didn’t appear to roll out the welcome mat.

Kelly offered a nervous smile and allowed Ryan to seat her. This was going to be a long night.

“How are you, Kelly?” Devon asked politely.

He was seated next to her and she supposed common courtesy dictated his question.

"I'm good," she replied in a low voice. "Nervous."

He seemed surprised by her honesty.

Ryan conversed with his friends and his mother. Kelly sat quietly beside him and watched the goings-on around her. No one tried to include her in conversation and the one time she offered a comment, the awkward silence that ensued told her all she needed to know.

They were tolerating her for Ryan's sake, but she didn't miss the looks they cast in his direction when they thought she wasn't watching. Looks that plainly said, *Are you crazy?*

By the time the food was served, she was extremely grateful to have something to focus on. She felt out of place. She felt conspicuous. This was going down as one of the worst nights of her life and she was counting the minutes until she and Ryan could make their escape.

The food felt dry in her mouth. Her stomach churned and after only a few bites, she gave up trying to force herself to eat. Instead, she sipped at her water and pretended she was back on the beach with Ryan, about to dance underneath the moonlight.

That was her problem. She was living in a fantasy world, avoiding reality. And reality sucked. Her reality was sitting here at a dinner table while five other people judged her. Her reality was living with a man—a man she intended to marry—who felt he needed to forgive her for sins she hadn't committed.

At what point in her life had she decided she didn't deserve better than this?

It was a startling discovery. The blinders had come off.

Why was she putting up with this?

She was prepared to end the entire thing when she looked up and saw Jarrod walk to the table. He leaned over and kissed his mom then held up a hand in greeting to the others before turning his gaze on her and Ryan.

She broke into a cold sweat. Ryan stiffened beside her and the others fell silent.

It was as if everyone in the room waited for the inevitable fireworks. Her head pounded viciously. Her stomach cramped and she wanted to die from the humiliation. More than that, she was so furious she couldn't see straight.

"Sorry, I'm late," he said. "I got caught in traffic."

As he took the empty chair beside his mother, bile rose in Kelly's throat. Her heart was shredded. She was bleeding on the inside, so hurt, so devastated she wanted to die. She refused to look at Ryan. How could he have done it? She didn't believe for a moment that Ryan had actually invited his brother…had he? But why hadn't he made it clear that he wasn't welcome?

Everyone stared at her. They likely thought she deserved whatever humiliation was heaped upon her tonight. But she refused to look back at them. She wouldn't give them the satisfaction of seeing her so shattered.

Instead her gaze locked onto Jarrod Beardsley and his mother.

How they must hate her. The coldness in Ramona Beardsley's eyes reached out to Kelly. They said, *You'll never win. I'll never let you.*

What had she ever done besides love Ryan? Enough was enough.

Kelly deserved better.

She was through paying penance.

She was done with being looked down on, condemned and *forgiven.*

Forcing a smile in Ryan's direction, she pushed back her chair and slowly rose as if she hadn't a care in the world. She stared across the table at Jarrod and his mother and let the full force of her hatred shine. She didn't care if they ever accepted her. She didn't accept them. They could both go to hell. She'd buy them a first-class ticket.

Then she turned to face the entire table. "I'm done here. You've all sat and stared your disapproval. You've sent pitying glances Ryan's way. You've judged me and found me not good enough. To hell with all of you."

Then she turned back to Jarrod, her voice coming out in a low hiss. "You son of a bitch. You stay away from me and my child. I'll see you in hell before I ever let you near me again."

Ryan started to rise, but she shoved him back into his seat. "By all means, you stay. You wouldn't want to disappoint your family and friends."

Before he could react, she stalked away.

She bypassed the doorway leading to the bathrooms and kept on walking. She burst into the cold, shivering because she hadn't bothered to collect her coat. She embraced the chill, welcomed the cold slap in the face.

Her head had ached all afternoon, but after spending the past hour with her teeth gritted and her jaw tight, the headache had exploded into vicious pain.

She walked a block before the cold penetrated the thin layers of her dress. She stopped and waved at a passing cab but it didn't stop. It took two more attempts before she managed to get one to pull over for her.

She was barely able to get out Ryan's address before the tears started to fall.

Ryan's first thought was to go after Kelly, but he was furious, and this had to be ended now. Like hell he'd ever allow anyone to make Kelly feel the way she'd obviously felt tonight. He bolted to his feet, palms smacking the table as he lunged toward his brother.

"What the hell was that?"

He included his mother in his furious gaze, not backing down when she recoiled from his anger.

Jarrod looked taken aback, his face pale. He looked sick, but at this point Ryan didn't care. He'd had enough. This was a huge mistake and he wasn't going to let it go this time. He never should have let it go. Never should have played down the obvious discord between Kelly and his family.

Their mother leaned forward, her expression tight. "Don't be angry with him, Ryan. I invited him. If you insist on a relationship with this woman we're going to have to sit down together at some point. Or do you plan never to see your family? Hasn't she caused us enough pain?"

Ryan let out a curse that made his mother flinch. "Haven't you hurt her enough? It ends tonight. I'm done with this. I'm done subjecting Kelly to your insensitivity and your blatant attempts to drive us apart."

Then he turned in his friends' direction. "Rafael, it was good to see you and Bryony again. I hope to see you before you leave the city."

He nodded at Devon and Cam, who looked as if they'd rather be anyplace but where they were. That made three of them.

"Sorry, man," Devon murmured.

Not sparing his mother or brother a second glance, Ryan left the table and went in search of Kelly, hoping she hadn't made it past the door yet. He'd take her home, apologize profusely and then he'd promise that he wouldn't subject her to another gathering of his friends and family.

He shouldn't have this time but he'd hoped… He wasn't sure what he'd hoped but he'd been a damn fool and he'd hurt Kelly in the process.

He stalked toward the coatroom, but found Kelly's coat still hanging. Then he hurried toward the entrance, but found no sign of her there either. Dread tightened his gut.

"Did you see a pregnant woman leave? Short, blond, wearing a blue dress?" he demanded of the maître d'.

"Yes, sir. She walked out just a few seconds ago."

Ryan swore. "Did you see which way she went?"

"No, I'm sorry, but you might ask outside to see if anyone got her a cab."

Ryan hurried into the night, praying she'd gone home. But what if she hadn't? What if she'd finally had enough and said to hell with him and everyone else?

After being told that Kelly was seen walking down the street, Ryan panicked and took off at a run. Fear lanced through him at the idea of her being out alone, upset, on her feet when she had no business walking such a distance.

He brushed by countless people and then he saw her just ahead, getting into a cab at the next block. He yelled her name, but the door shut and the cab drove off—leaving him standing on the sidewalk, his heart about to explode out of his chest.

He waved at a passing cab, frustrated when it didn't slow. The next one stopped and he climbed in, directing the driver to his address. The entire way back to his apartment he prayed that she'd be there.

When the cab pulled up to his apartment building, he got out and hurried toward the door. When he reached the doorman, he stopped.

"Did you see Miss Christian come in a few minutes ago?"

The doorman nodded. "Yes, sir. She got here just before you arrived."

Relief staggered him. He bolted for the elevator. A few moments later, he strode into the apartment.

"Kelly? Kelly, honey, where are you?"

Not waiting for an answer, he hurried into the bedroom to see her sitting on the edge of the bed, her face pale and drawn in pain. When she heard him, she looked up and he winced at the dullness in her eyes.

She'd been crying.

"I thought I could do it," she said in a raw voice, before he could beg her forgiveness. "I thought I could just go on and forget and that I could accept others thinking the worst of me as long as you and I were okay again. I did myself a huge disservice."

"Kelly..."

Something in her look silenced him and he stood several feet away, a feeling of helplessness gripping him as he watched her try to compose herself.

"I sat there tonight while your friends and your mother looked at me in disgust, while they looked at you with a mixture of pity and disbelief in their eyes. All because you took me back. The tramp who betrayed you in the worst possible manner. And I thought to myself I don't deserve this. I've *never* deserved it. I deserve better."

She raised her eyes to his and he flinched at the horrible pain he saw reflected there. Then she laughed. A raw, terrible sound that grated across his ears.

"And earlier tonight you forgave me. You stood there and told me it no longer mattered what happened in the past because you *forgave* me and you wanted to move forward."

She curled her fingers into tight balls and rage

flared in her eyes. She stood and stared him down even as tears ran in endless streams down her cheeks.

"Well, I don't forgive *you.* Nor can I forget that you betrayed me in the worst way a man can betray the woman he's supposed to love and be sworn to protect."

He took a step back, reeling from the fury in her voice. His eyes narrowed. "You don't forgive *me?*"

"I told you the truth that day," she said hoarsely, her voice cracking under the weight of her tears. "I begged you to believe me. I got down on my knees and *begged* you. And what did you do? You wrote me a damn check and told me to get out."

He took another step back, his hand going to his hair. Something was wrong, terribly wrong. So much of that day was a blur. He remembered her on her knees, her tear-stained face, how she put her hand on his leg and whispered, "Please don't do this."

It made him sick. He never wanted to go back to the way he felt that day, but somehow this was worse because there was something terribly wrong in her eyes and in her voice.

"Your brother *assaulted* me. He *forced* himself on me. I didn't invite his attentions. I wore the bruises from his attack for two weeks. *Two weeks.* I was so stunned by what he'd done that all I could think about was getting to you. I knew you'd fix it. You'd protect me. You'd take care of me. I knew you'd make it right. All I could think about was running to you. And, oh God, I did and you looked right through me."

The sick knot in his stomach grew and his chest tightened so much he couldn't breathe.

"You wouldn't listen," she said tearfully. "You wouldn't listen to anything I had to say. You'd already made your mind up."

He swallowed and closed the distance between them, worried that she'd fall if he didn't make her sit. But she shook him off and turned her back, her shoulders heaving as her quiet sobs fell over the room.

"I'm listening now, Kelly," he forced out. "Tell me what happened. I'll believe you. I swear."

But he knew. He already knew. So much of

that day was replaying over and over in his head and suddenly he was able to see so clearly what he'd refused to see before.

And it was killing him.

His brother had lied to him after all. Not just lied but he'd carefully orchestrated the truth and twisted it so cleverly that Ryan had been completely deceived.

Then she turned, her beautiful eyes haunted, defeated. "It doesn't matter if you believe me anymore," she whispered. "You wouldn't believe me when it *mattered.* He tried to rape me. He assaulted me. He touched me. He hurt me. And when I fought him off and told him that I would tell you what he'd done, he told me he'd make sure you never believed a word of any of it.

"And you know what the funny thing is? I told him he was wrong. I told him that you l-loved me and that you would make him pay for hurting me."

She broke off as another sob racked her.

Oh God. Oh God. What had he done? He remembered the phone call from his brother as though it was yesterday. He hadn't believed him.

At first. Not until Kelly had arrived in an agitated state telling him the exact same story that Jarrod had just told him over the phone.

"He told you the truth," Kelly said scornfully as if she'd plucked the thoughts right out of his head. "He told you *exactly* what happened, only he said that it was all a *lie,* that I made it up because I didn't want you to know what really supposedly happened. He wanted to make sure that when I ran to you and told you what happened that you wouldn't believe a word. And how better to do that than to tell you that I would *claim* to be attacked, that I'd *claim* he tried to rape me."

Ryan stared at her in horror as the realization of what had really happened that day hit him.

"And sure enough. I run straight to you and tell you that your precious brother just tried to rape me and you look at me with those cold eyes and call me a liar. All because he told you that's what I'd say."

"Did he?" Ryan asked in a near whisper. "Did he rape you, Kelly?"

"He *touched* me. He touched me in a way that

only you were allowed to touch me. He hit me. He bruised me. Isn't that enough?" she asked in a hysterical voice. "The irony in all of this is that you were so worried I was pregnant with his baby. We never had sex though God knows he tried."

She broke off again and buried her face in her hands. He wanted to go to her, take her in his arms, but he was afraid that just as he'd rejected her before, so would she reject him now.

She yanked her hands down, her face ragged and ravaged by grief, the same grief that was tearing through him.

"I should have been able to come to you," she whispered. "Of all the people in the world, you should have been the one to believe in me. And I just can't get past that. You should have been the one to hold me and tell me it would be all right. I was so excited that day. I took a pregnancy test that morning and found out I was pregnant. I was so excited and nervous. So worried about how you'd react. But so thrilled that I was pregnant with your child."

She broke off again, sobs tearing from her

throat. She buried her face in her hands as her shoulders shook violently.

"Kelly, I'm so sorry. I thought… He was my *brother.* I never considered he would do something like that. He'd never shown any animosity toward you. He'd never been anything but accepting of you. The two of you seemed to get along well. I never dreamed he'd do something that despicable."

She raised her head and stared at him with dull eyes. "But you thought I would."

The sudden silence was damning. He stared at her, completely frozen. He had no defense because at the time he'd believed *Jarrod.* He'd made his choice and it hadn't been Kelly. Even when she'd begged him. She'd told him the truth. She'd come to him for protection. She'd come to him hurt and afraid. And he'd thrown her out after making her feel like a whore. All because he couldn't imagine his own flesh and blood committing such an atrocity. It had appeared to him that it was everything Jarrod said it was, a ridiculous accusation to hide the sin of her infidelity.

His eyes burned. His throat swelled and knotted. For the first time in his life he was faced with a situation where he had no idea what to do. She had every right to hate him.

She put a hand to her head and rubbed. She swayed and then bent over as if she was about to fall.

"Kelly!"

He went forward, but she jerked upright again and thrust out a hand to ward him off.

"Just stay away," she said in a low, desperate voice.

"Kelly, please."

It was his turn to beg. And God, he would. He'd do anything to make her stay long enough that he could make it up to her.

"I love you. I never stopped loving you."

She lifted her gaze again, her eyes drenched with tears—and pain. "*Love* isn't supposed to hurt this much. Love isn't this. Love is trust."

He moved forward again, so desperate to hold her, to offer the comfort he had denied her when she'd needed him most. Anger and sorrow vied for control. Grief welled in his chest until he thought he might explode. Rage surged through his veins like acid.

She put her hand to her head again and started to walk past him. He caught at her elbow, anything to stop her, because he knew in his heart she was going to walk away. He didn't deserve a second chance. He didn't deserve for her to stay. He didn't deserve her love. But he wanted it. He wanted it more than he wanted to live.

"Please don't go."

She turned back to him, sadness so deep in her gaze that it hurt him to look at her. "Don't you see, Ryan? It can never work for us. You don't trust me. Your family and friends hate me. What kind of life will that be for me? I deserve more than that. It's taken me long enough to figure that out. I settled again, when I swore I'd never do it. I agreed to marry you. Again. Because I was so in love with you and I believed that we could move forward. But I was a fool. Some obstacles are insurmountable."

She closed her eyes as another spasm of pain crossed her face. And she swayed, her hand flying out to brace herself against the dresser.

"Kelly, what's wrong?" he demanded.

She rubbed her hand across her brow and opened her eyes, but her stare was unfocused. "My head." A sound like a whimper escaped her and he knew that something was wrong. Something beyond the emotional distress she was experiencing.

Her face took on a gray pallor that alarmed him. Panic flared in her eyes and just for a moment she looked to him for help.

Before he could react, her knees buckled and she slid soundlessly to the floor.

Sixteen

"Kelly!"

Ryan dropped to the floor. His immediate reaction was to gather her in his arms, but she was rigid and her body convulsed. Light foam gathered at her lips and her jaw was tight. Frantically he reached for his phone and clumsily punched 911.

"I need an ambulance," he said tersely. "My fiancée. She's pregnant. I think she's having a seizure." He knew he didn't make sense. His heart and mind were screaming even as he tried to stay calm. The 911 operator asked questions and he answered them mechanically as he leaned over Kelly, desperate to help her.

After a moment her body went slack and her head lolled to the side. He put his fingers to her neck, praying that he'd find a pulse. He laid his head over her chest, listening and feeling for air exchange.

"Don't leave me, Kelly," he whispered desperately. "Please hang on. I love you so damn much."

He lifted her limp hand, the one that bore his ring and pressed her palm to his cheek. He kissed the skin, his breaths coming in ragged, silent sobs. He'd never been more scared in his life.

The minutes dragged to eternity. The operator continued to ask him questions and offered him encouragement. But Kelly remained unconscious and the longer she lay there, still, on the floor, the more his panic and sense of helplessness grew.

After what seemed an interminable wait, he heard the EMS crew call out from the door.

"In here!" he called hoarsely.

They hurried in, motioning him away from Kelly as they began to administer care. Through it all, Ryan stood there numbly, watching as they lifted her onto a stretcher and hurried toward the elevator.

He followed behind, whispered prayers falling from his lips. They loaded her onto the waiting ambulance and he climbed in behind her.

Halfway to the hospital, he pulled out his phone but then stared blankly down at it. Who would he call? There was no one. Cold fury iced his veins. The very people he'd trusted—especially his brother—had acted unforgivably. Until now he'd never really experienced true hatred.

He buried his face in his hands and willed himself not to lose his composure. Not now. Kelly needed him. He hadn't been there for her before. He'd already made the mistake of abandoning her when she'd needed him the absolute most.

Now he'd die before he ever allowed her to think she wasn't the most important thing in the world to him.

Ryan stood listening to the doctor tell him that Kelly's condition was indeed serious. She was on a magnesium sulfate drip to lower her blood pressure and prevent future seizures, but if she didn't respond in the next few hours an emergency C-section would have to be performed.

"And the risks to the child?" Ryan croaked. "It's too soon, isn't it?"

The doctor gave him a look of sympathy. "We won't have a choice. If left untreated, both mother and child could die. The only cure for eclampsia is delivery of the baby. We're doing tests to determine the lung maturity of the baby. At thirty-four weeks' gestation, the child has a very good chance of survival without complications."

Ryan dug a hand into his hair and closed his eyes. He'd done this to her. She should have been cherished and pampered during her entire pregnancy. She should have been waited on hand and foot. Instead she'd been forced to work a physically demanding job under unimaginable stress. And once he'd brought her back, she'd been subjected to scorn and hostility and endless emotional distress.

Was it any wonder she wanted to wash her hands of him and his family?

"Will…will Kelly be all right? Will she recover from this?"

He didn't realize he held his breath until his chest began to burn. He let it out slowly and forced himself to relax his hands.

"She's gravely ill. Her blood pressure is extremely high. She could seize again or suffer a stroke. Neither is good for her or the baby. We're doing everything we can to bring her blood pressure down and we're monitoring the baby for signs of stress. We're prepared to take the baby if the condition of either mother or child deteriorates. It's important she remain calm and not be stressed in any way. Even if we're able to bring down her blood pressure and put off the delivery until closer to her due date, she'll be on strict bed rest for the remainder of her pregnancy."

"I understand," Ryan said quietly. "Can I see her now?"

"You can go in but she must remain calm. Don't do or say anything to upset her."

Ryan nodded and turned to walk the few steps

to Kelly's room. He paused at the door, afraid to go in. What if his mere presence upset her?

His hand rested on the handle and he leaned forward, pressing his forehead to the surface. He closed his eyes as grief and regret—so much regret—swamped him.

Finally he opened the door and eased inside. It was dark with only a light from the bathroom to illuminate the room. Kelly lay on the bed, a vast array of medical equipment on either side of her.

He approached cautiously, not wanting to disturb or upset her. He hovered by her side, staring down at her pale face. Her eyes were closed, but her brow was creased, whether in worry or pain he wasn't sure. Maybe both.

Her chest barely rose with the shallow breaths. Suddenly, everything that had happened tonight caught up to him in one painful rush.

Never. *Never* would he forget her grief-ravaged face as she bitterly told him what his brother had done to her, what she'd tried to tell him months before. But he hadn't listened then. He'd been convinced she was lying.

He pulled up a chair so he could sit as close to her as possible while she slept. Tentatively, he slid his fingers underneath the hand that didn't have an IV attached and he brought it to his lips, holding it against his mouth.

"I'm sorry, Kell," he said brokenly. "I'm so damn sorry."

"Ryan. Ryan, man, wake up."

The whisper stirred Ryan and he opened his eyes and groaned at the monster crick in his neck. Daylight streamed through the blinds on the window and he winced.

His gaze first found Kelly, who was still sleeping, her cheek resting on the mound of pillows. Her bed was elevated slightly so she wasn't lying flat and some time recently her IV bag had been replaced because it was now full.

Then he turned, his hand going to rub the kinks in his neck. Devon was standing next to the chair Ryan had slept in, his eyes dark with concern.

"What the hell happened?" Devon said in a low voice.

Carefully, Ryan stood, not wanting to risk waking Kelly up. He motioned for Dev to follow him outside the hospital room. When they walked out, Ryan saw Cam shove off the wall, his eyebrow arched in question.

"What are you two doing here?" Ryan asked with a frown.

"Last night was tense," Devon said. "We tried to call you but couldn't get you so we went by your apartment. Your doorman told us that Kelly had been taken to the hospital by ambulance so we came over to see if she's okay."

Ryan closed his eyes as his throat knotted all over again.

"Whoa, man, you need to sit down," Cam said. "Have you eaten?"

Ryan shook his head.

"Want to tell us about it?" Dev prompted.

Ryan stared at his two friends and emitted a harsh laugh. "How do you explain that you've made the worst mistake of your entire life and you're not sure you can ever make amends?"

"That bad, huh," Cam said.

"Worse."

"Is Kelly going to be all right?" Dev asked. "And the baby?"

"I wish I knew. They might have to deliver the baby early if her blood pressure doesn't go down. I did this to her. She's lying in a hospital bed because I wasn't there for her or my child. What kind of a bastard does that make me?"

Cam and Devon exchanged glances.

"Look, granted I don't know the whole story, but I'd say that you aren't solely to blame for the problem," Devon said carefully.

"My brother *assaulted* her," Ryan said as rage flooded him all over again. "He tried to rape her and when she fought him off, he called me with an ingenious story. He claimed they slept together but when he told her it was a mistake, she threatened to tell me he tried to rape her so I wouldn't break up with her for cheating on me. So of course not half an hour later when she shows up at my office telling me *exactly* what my brother said she would, I didn't believe her. Because I couldn't imagine my brother, the brother I all but raised, doing something so despicable. And when she begged me, when she got on her knees and *pleaded* with me to believe her, I wrote her a check and told her to get the hell out of my life."

Devon and Cam both looked at him stunned, speechless.

"How am I ever supposed to get past something like that," Ryan snarled. "Tell me how *she's* supposed to get past that. Do you know that just last night before dinner I magnanimously told her that I forgave her? That I wanted us to forget the past and move forward and that I *forgave* her for cheating on me."

He broke off and laughed a dry, harsh laugh.

"Yeah, from the start I've been all about being the bigger person and wanting to start over when all along I treated her so unforgivably. She came to me for help, for protection, because I was the one person she counted on, and I turned my back on her."

Ryan turned away as his composure slipped. Tears burned his eyes. Angry, furious tears. He wanted to ram his fist into the wall. He wanted to roar with rage.

His friends flanked him, each slipping a hand over his shoulder.

"I don't know what to say," Devon said quietly. "I know you love her."

"Yeah, I did, do, always have. I loved her and yet I did this to her. How is she ever going to be able to trust me again?"

"Someone needs to beat the hell out of that little bastard," Cam growled.

Ryan slowly raised his head, his face set in stone. "He'll never ever come close to her again. I'm going to kill him."

"Damn," Devon muttered. "Look, I know you're pissed and you have every right to be, but don't do anything stupid. He deserves to have his ass kicked, but don't do anything to land yourself in jail. Kelly needs you. You can't help her if you're behind bars."

"I can't let him get away with it," Ryan said. "He touched her. He violated her. He *hurt* her."

"I'm going with you," Cam said tersely.

Ryan shook his head.

"You don't get a choice. It's either I go with you or I'm calling the police. The difference is,

I'll let you beat the crap out of him. But I won't let you kill him. The police aren't going to let you touch him. So what'll it be?"

Ryan's lip curled into a snarl.

Devon sighed. "You should see yourself, man. It's a good thing Kelly is sleeping. Whatever it is you need to do, you need to get it done so that when she wakes up you can be the support she needs. You'll just scare her to death if she sees you like this."

"Devon can stay with Kelly," Cam volunteered. "I'll go with you to confront Jarrod. Then you can get your ass back here where you belong and put this whole thing behind you."

Cam made it sound easy, but Ryan knew better. Kelly might not ever forgive him and he wouldn't blame her if she didn't. But if she did and if she and Ryan were going to be together, he was going to make damn sure his family was never an issue for her again.

"Will you do it?" Ryan asked. "Will you stay with her for a while? If she wakes let her know…"

"I'll handle it," Devon said. "You just go so you can get your head on straight again. And rip his nuts off for me. The bastard deserves it."

Seventeen

Jarrod's expression was one of resignation when he opened the door to Ryan's insistent knock. Ryan didn't give him time to do or say anything. He grabbed his brother by the shirt and propelled him backward into the small studio apartment Jarrod lived in.

"What the—?"

Ryan silenced him with a fist. Jarrod went sprawling and Ryan and Cam both stood a few feet back waiting for him to pick himself up off the floor.

Jarrod wiped at the blood on his mouth as he stumbled to his feet. "What the hell, Ryan?"

"Why did you do it?" Ryan asked in a deadly quiet voice. *"Why?"*

An uneasy expression crawled across Jarrod's face. His lips drooped and his eyes went dull. At least he wasn't going to pretend he didn't know what Ryan was talking about.

Jarrod dragged a hand across his mouth again, his hand coming away smeared with blood. "I know it won't mean much, but I'm sorry."

Ryan exploded at him. Jarrod didn't even try to defend himself. He went down on the floor and this time he didn't get up.

"Sorry? You're *sorry?* You tried to rape her. You lied to me about her. What the hell is wrong with you? She was the woman I was going to marry. Why would you do something like that?"

"Mom," Jarrod said in a weary voice.

Ryan took a step back, stunned. "Mom? *Mom* put you up to this?"

Jarrod dragged himself only up enough to lean against the living room wall and he put a hand through his hair, his expression weary and defeated.

"Yeah. She went ballistic when she found out you proposed to Kelly. She was determined you weren't going to marry some penniless upstart. Her words not mine. I thought she was crazy at first. I mean I figured she'd throw a fit and then get over it, but then she wanted me to go buy her off. She said that if Kelly refused the offer, I should frame her with the fake rape story. I swear to you I wouldn't have raped her, Ryan. I just wanted to set it up so you'd think we slept together."

"Jesus," Cam muttered. "This is crazy."

Ryan was numb from head to toe. His own mother had done something that sick? It didn't seem possible. How could anyone hate someone else so much that they'd go to such lengths to get rid of them?

"She invited me to dinner last night. But I swear, Ryan, she told me that *you* wanted me there, that you and Kelly wanted to let the past go and start over. I wasn't going to go, because I didn't want to upset Kelly or make you angry, but Mom told me you specifically asked for me to come. And I hoped… I hoped that maybe you and Kelly could forgive the past and that we could be a family again. Like old times."

Ryan dropped his hands to his sides, suddenly so sick at heart that he just wanted to walk away. "You're no longer my family. Kelly and our child are my family. I don't *ever* want to see you again. If I ever catch you near Kelly I swear to you that you'll regret it."

"Ryan, don't. Please," Jarrod called hoarsely.

Ryan stopped at the door and slowly turned around. "Did she beg you like you're begging me, Jarrod? Did she ask you to stop?"

Jarrod's face flushed a dull red and then he looked away, no longer able to meet his brother's gaze.

"Come on," Cam said quietly. "Let's go, man."

As they walked back out, Ryan nudged Cam toward the waiting car. "You go. I'll take a cab. I'm going to see my mother."

Cam hesitated. "Sure you don't want me to go with you?"

"Yeah. This is something I have to do by myself."

* * *

Ryan knocked tersely on the door to his mother's home and issued a clipped demand to see her when one of the maids answered the door.

A moment later, as he paced the floor of the receiving room, his mother hurried in, her brow wrinkled in concern.

"Ryan? Is something wrong? You didn't call to tell me you were coming."

He stared at her, wondering how he could be so blind about the woman who'd given birth to him. There was no doubt she'd always been self-centered, but he'd never considered her malicious enough to harm an innocent woman.

Even now, after everything that had happened, he was at a loss for words. How could he possibly convey the depth of his hatred? It boiled in his veins like acid. His family. The people he should be able to count on. They were…evil.

The irony struck him hard. Kelly should have been able to count on him. But just as his family had betrayed him, he had betrayed Kelly. Maybe he was more like his mother and brother than he wanted to admit. The thought sickened him.

"Ryan?" she asked again.

She stopped in front of him and put her hand on his arm, her eyes worried.

He wiped her hand away and took a step back, choking on his disgust.

"Don't touch me," he said in a low voice. "I know what you did. I know what you and Jarrod did. I'll never forgive you for it."

Her face creased with consternation. She threw up her hand and turned away, her arms crossing over her chest.

"She's not who you should be with, Ryan. If you weren't so infatuated with her, so blinded by…lust, you'd see it too."

"You're not even going to deny it. My God. What did Kelly ever do to deserve what you did to her? She's lying in a hospital right now. She carries my child, *your* grandchild. She was pregnant when you sent Jarrod to attack her. What kind of a psychopath does that kind of thing?"

"I don't regret protecting my sons," she said stiffly. "I'd do it again. You'll understand when your son or daughter is born. You'll understand why I did what I did. With parenthood comes the knowledge that you'll do anything at all for your child. You'll protect them with everything you have. You can't just stand by and let your child make the worst mistake of their life and do nothing. Come talk to me in a few years. Then ask yourself if you still hate me so much."

He was dumbfounded by the lengths she went to justify her actions. They weren't simply morally reprehensible. They were criminal!

"I would hope that I never act as you have, that I'd never hurt an innocent woman just because I didn't think she was good enough. Here's what you don't understand, Mother. She's a better person than you'll ever be. Not good enough? We aren't good enough for her. We'll never be. I just have to hope to hell she'll accept and forgive me despite the worthless excuse for a family that I have."

His mother's eyes burned with outrage. "You're a typical man. Thinking with the lower portion of your anatomy. You're completely blinded by lust, but in a few years you won't look at her with the same lovesick puppy eyes. Then you'll thank me for trying to protect you. You can do better than her, Ryan. Why can't I make you see that?"

Ryan shook his head, sadness and grief so thick in his chest he could barely breathe. "I'll never thank you for this. You're nothing to me anymore. I'll never subject my wife or children to your poison."

Her face whitened with shock. "You don't mean that!"

"I mean it. You aren't my mother. I have no mother. I have no family save Kelly and our child. I'll never forgive you for this. Stay away from me. Stay away from Kelly. If you ever come within a hundred yards of my family, I'll forget that you gave birth to me and I'll have you hauled away in handcuffs. Are we understood?"

She stared wordlessly at him, suddenly looking every one of her sixty years. If she hadn't so callously tried to destroy the woman he loved, he would have felt sorry for her. But she showed no remorse. No regret.

"I have nothing more to say to you," he bit out.

He turned and walked away, his mother's cries for him to stop ringing in his ears.

He walked out of her house, never looking back. He got into the waiting cab and directed the driver back to the hospital. Kelly needed him. Their child needed him.

Chances were she'd never forgive him, but he'd make sure she never wanted for another thing in her life. He'd provide for her and their child. He'd spend the rest of his life making it up to her if only she'd let him.

Kelly awoke to silence. She was so relieved to no longer hear the horrible ringing in her ears that she could weep. The vile headache was gone. It no longer felt like the top of her head was going to explode.

She was oddly free of pain.

It took her several moments of staring at her surroundings to discover that she was in a hospital room.

Then the events leading up to her collapse came back to her in a flash. Her hands flew automatically to her belly and she was only partially reassured to feel the tight ball there. Was her baby okay? Was she herself okay?

She blinked harder to bring the room more into focus. There was light shining through a crack in the bathroom door. A glance at the blinds told her that it was dark outside.

Then her gaze fell on the chair beside her bed and she found Ryan staring at her, his gaze intense. She flinched away from the raw emotion shining in his blue eyes.

"Hey," he said quietly. "How are you feeling?"

"Numb," she answered before she could think better of it. "Kind of blank. My head doesn't hurt anymore. Are my feet still swollen?"

He carefully picked up the sheet and pushed it over her feet. "Maybe a little. Not as bad as they were. They've been giving you meds and they're monitoring the baby."

"How is she?" Kelly asked, a knot of fear in her throat.

"For now, she's doing fine. Your blood pressure stabilized, but they might have to do a C-section if it goes back up or if the baby starts showing signs of distress."

Kelly closed her eyes and then suddenly Ryan

was close to her, holding her, his lips pressed against her temple.

"Don't worry, love," he murmured. "You're supposed to stay calm. You're getting the best possible care. I've made sure of it. They're monitoring you round-the-clock. And the doctor said the baby has an excellent prognosis at thirty-four weeks' gestation."

She sagged against the pillow and closed her eyes. Relief pulsed through her but she was so tired she couldn't muster the energy to do anything more than lie there thanking God that her baby was okay.

"I'm going to take care of you, Kell," Ryan said softly against her temple. "You and our baby. Nothing will ever hurt you again. I swear it."

Tears burned her eyelids. She was emotionally and physically exhausted and didn't have the strength to argue. Something inside her was broken and she had no idea how to fix it. She felt so…disconnected.

Ryan drew away, but his eyes were bright with concern…and love. But was it enough? What was love without trust? He wanted her. He felt guilty. He wasn't a jerk. He had feelings and it would destroy him now that he knew the truth. But he hadn't trusted her, and Kelly wasn't sure if they could even forge a relationship when this much hurt and betrayal was involved. Maybe they'd been stupid to even attempt it.

"What's going to happen?" she whispered. "Do I have to stay here? Do I go home?" She bit her lip because she wasn't sure where she'd go. Her relationship with Ryan was a big question mark, but she had no place to go except home with him. And her baby's health came first.

He took her hand—the one that she wore his ring on—and thumbed it absently.

"You'll stay here until a decision is made about your health. But the doctor said that if you go home, you'll be on strict bed rest for the rest of your pregnancy."

Her expression must have reflected her horror and her fear, because Ryan leaned over to kiss her forehead again. He held her hand and rubbed his thumb over her knuckles.

"I don't want you to worry, honey, okay? I'll handle everything. We'll go someplace warm and beautiful and all you'll have to do is lie on the beach or in a comfortable chair and watch the sun set. I'll hire a personal physician to oversee every part of your care."

Her brow furrowed and she could feel the pain creep back into her head.

"Ryan, we can't just go off to some island paradise somewhere. Ignoring our problems won't fix them."

He stroked a hand over her forehead, smoothing her hair back. "Right now, all you need to concentrate on is feeling better and carrying our child for as long as you can. And what I need to concentrate on is removing as much stress from your life as possible."

She opened her mouth to respond, but he kissed her lightly, silencing her.

"I know we have a lot to work out, Kell. I had no idea how much when I said this before. But right now let's put our differences aside and concentrate on our baby and your health. Can we do that?"

Her resistance slid away. She nodded slowly, not withdrawing her hand from his.

Despite what had happened in the past, she didn't doubt for a moment that he cared deeply about her and their baby. And he was right. No matter what had to be worked out between them, their child came first.

Eighteen

"I'm reluctant to release Miss Christian from the hospital," Kelly's doctor said grimly as he stood outside her hospital room. "She's shown marked improvement. Her blood pressure is normal. The baby is showing no signs of fetal distress. I'd say she has a good chance of carrying the child the full forty weeks. But I'm not comfortable releasing her yet."

Ryan rubbed the back of his neck. "What can I do to make it possible? She's unhappy here. She's not herself."

The doctor nodded. "That's precisely why I'm concerned about releasing her. At least here I can be assured she's getting the care she needs. She's not in good spirits and I'm deeply concerned about her stress level. It's imperative that she not be placed in any situation that causes her undue distress."

"If you give her the okay to travel I plan to take her away. Someplace warm where she'll never have to lift a finger. I can have a medical team fly us to the island and once there, I'll have a private physician to monitor her care as well as have the local hospital completely apprised of her condition and needs."

The doctor went silent as he seemed to mull over Ryan's suggestion. "Perhaps that's the best idea. It's cold and a bit gloomy right now. Maybe the better weather will lift her spirits and she'll regain her strength. It's not good for her or the baby if she gives birth now when she's verging on depression."

It made Ryan's heart ache to think of Kelly being sad and depressed. He'd do anything at all to make her smile again.

"Give me your okay and I'll make immediate arrangements for us to leave the city," Ryan said quietly. "I want only the best for her and I'll do whatever it takes to make her well again."

The doctor stared hard at him and then lowered his clipboard to his waist. "I believe you, Mr. Beardsley. Tell you what. You give me the name of the physician you hire as well as the name of the hospital that will be overseeing her care and I'll have her medical records transferred. I'll want to talk to her physician personally and make sure he's aware of the severity and the complexity of the situation. I'll also want to make sure the hospital is prepared to take the baby at the first sign of distress. And that they have adequately trained personnel for this situation."

"Thank you," Ryan said sincerely. "Kelly and I both appreciate your attention in this matter."

"Just take good care of her. I hate to see the young lady so sad."

Ryan nodded, his chest tight. He'd take good care of her, no doubt, but it remained to be seen if he could make her happy again. Still, he wasn't about to give up. He'd turned his back on her once. Never again would she have any cause to doubt him. If it took him forever, he'd make damn sure she knew she could count on him.

Kelly sat in the armchair by the window in her hospital room and stared out as snowflakes drifted down in crazy little spirals. Though it was plenty warm in her room, a chill crept over her shoulders and she shivered.

"Do you want a blanket?" Ryan asked.

She turned her head in surprise. She hadn't expected him back, though she should have known he wouldn't be gone for long. He'd been a constant presence over the past few days, always there, anticipating her every need.

"Sorry if I startled you," he said in a low voice.

"You didn't. I just didn't hear you come in."

He moved in front of her and perched on the windowsill. He shoved his hands in his pockets and then leveled a stare at her.

"I just finished talking to your doctor. He's willing to release you."

Her eyes widened in surprise.

"There are conditions, of course. He's very concerned over your health."

She frowned. "What conditions?"

"I've already made all the arrangements. I've taken care of everything. There's nothing you need to worry about. Just concentrate on getting well and regaining your strength."

She shook her head, trying to clear some of the constant fuzz that seemed to permeate her brain lately. She'd existed in a fog ever since her collapse, and worse, her fatigue had grown worse. Something inside stirred, though, as though she ought to protest, but she couldn't summon the mental energy to do it.

When she remained silent, Ryan continued on. "We're leaving the city. An ambulance is going to transport you to the airport where a medical team is going to fly us to St. Angelo."

Again she shook her head in silent denial. And she finally found her objection.

"Ryan, you can't just leave here. It could be weeks before I have the baby. You can't hover over me for so long. Neither can you leave your work. Your life is *here*."

He slid to his knees in front of her and gathered her hands in his. "My life is with *you*. You and our baby are my absolute priority. I have people who are more than capable of running things in my absence. I have business partners who are more than willing to step in and take over any matters needing my attention. We'll be minutes from the resort construction site, so I can easily oversee any issues that arise there."

Nothing had been said of the night she'd collapsed after her emotional breakdown. It had been a carefully avoided issue, as was the matter of their future…and his brother. She could see the torment and the terrible guilt in Ryan's eyes, but he didn't broach the subject and neither did she. She couldn't do it without upsetting herself and, above all else, the doctor had warned her against becoming distressed. She couldn't afford another complete loss of control like the night she'd ended up in the hospital.

So she'd locked everything behind an impenetrable wall of ice and indifference. Any time she felt her emotions rising, she turned them off and didn't offer objection or resistance.

And she'd do the same now. Her heart told her to object, to not allow him to take over and whisk her away. She was tired of being hurt. But it simply took too much effort and she'd expended all of her strength.

"Kelly?" he asked softly. "What are you thinking, honey?"

She moved her gaze until it rested on him. His brow was creased in concern and he was staring hard at her as if he was trying to reach in and pluck out her thoughts.

"I'm tired," she said honestly. And weak. Heartsick. Unsure of what she wanted. Battling over what was best for her baby.

So many things that she wouldn't admit because it simply took too much effort to explain.

He touched her cheek, caressing gently. "I know you are, baby. I have no right to ask this of you, but I'm asking anyway. Trust me. Let me take care of you. Let me take you away. You loved it on the island."

How easy he made it for her to cede control. He was offering her everything she'd ever wanted. His love. His care. Fantasy. He was offering her a fantasy. But fantasies never lasted. They'd already done this once. Escaped from reality for a few idyllic days on the island, but when it was all over they'd had to return to the cold reality of their lives.

"I want to stay there until I have the baby," she said quietly. She didn't want her baby born here. She didn't want to be surrounded by people who despised her. She didn't want her child exposed to the animosity she herself had been a victim of.

"Already arranged."

Her eyes widened in surprise.

"Come with me, Kell. Trust me. At least for now."

Maybe she could stay on the island after the baby was born. Surely Ryan saw the impossibility of them having a relationship by now. But she and the baby could live there. They wouldn't need much. A small cottage or even an apartment. As soon as she was back on her feet, she could find work. She'd waitressed. She wasn't afraid of hard work.

And when Ryan wanted to see their child he could come to the island. For a man with his own jet and a resort that would be completed within a year, it wouldn't be a hardship to visit his child often.

Encouraged by having a goal, a plan, she nodded.

Ryan's relief was palpable. He leaned forward to kiss her, but she turned her head so that his mouth glanced off her cheek instead.

"I have to leave for just a little while," he said when he pulled back. "I need to finalize all the arrangements for our departure and make sure your needs will be met for the entire trip. I'll be back as soon as I can. Is there anything I can bring you?"

She shook her head and he rose but before he walked away, he stroked a hand over her hair. "I'll do anything to make you smile again, Kell."

Before she could respond, he turned and walked quietly from the room, leaving her to stare out the window as it snowed.

The flight and subsequent transportation to the villa on the beach was seamless. Ryan had ensured that she was given every consideration. She was endlessly pampered and waited on and when they arrived on the island, they were greeted not only by the physician who would be monitoring her care, but a personal nurse who would reside at the villa with her and Ryan.

When Kelly got her first look at the sprawling villa, it took her breath away. They drove through a gate and down a winding driveway that was lined with lush, gorgeous flowers. Just for a moment the driveway paralleled the beach before it ended in front of the main house.

The house couldn't be more than a few steps from the beach. The idea that she could walk out the back door and be on the sand sent excitement coursing through her veins.

Ryan insisted on carrying her inside. He cradled her close as he walked through the front door and she craned her neck to take in the interior.

Instead of showing her around, he took her to the glass doors that led to the wraparound porch in the back. As she had suspected, there were only three stones marking the very short pathway from the porch to the sand.

As soon as she stepped onto the porch, the

breeze from the water ruffled her hair. She closed her eyes and inhaled deeply, savoring the tang of the salt and the lush, warm air that surrounded them.

"It's beautiful," she breathed.

He smiled. "I'm glad you approve—because it's yours."

She went still in his arms and locked her gaze with his. For a long moment she was too stunned to find her voice. When she finally did, it came out as a croak. "I don't understand."

He eased her down onto the steps leading to the sand. Then he sat beside her as they stared over the shimmering blue of the water.

"I bought it for you. For us. This is your house."

She was at a complete loss for words. The numbness that she'd worn for so long was melting away. It was as if the warmth of the sun was thawing the ice and with it, brought new awareness. She saw things more clearly. She saw Ryan. She saw him making a huge effort to make her happy. To take care of her. Hope began to beat inside her chest, but she pushed it back, afraid to give it free rein. She didn't dare make assumptions.

"But Ryan, you live in New York. Your life is there. Your family is there. Your job, your business, your friends. You can't just move here because we had a few days of happiness."

"Can't I?" he challenged.

He picked up her hand and laced his fingers through hers. "There's a lot you don't know, Kelly. I didn't want you to know at the time. You were dealing with enough stress in the hospital. I've cut my brother and my mother out of my life. Out of *our* lives."

"Oh, Ryan." Tears swam in her eyes. No matter how much she despised them, she had never wanted this for him.

He wiped a tear away with his thumb. "Don't you dare shed a tear for them or for me. They aren't worth your tears. I don't regret what I've done. I only regret that I allowed them to hurt you and that I never saw what they were doing to you."

"But you wouldn't have done it if it weren't for me," she said painfully. "They're your family,

Ryan. Maybe you're angry with them now, but what about a year from now? Or five years from now? At what point will you resent me for being the wedge between you?"

"You aren't responsible for their actions," he said fiercely. "You didn't do this. They did. No one else. I hate them for what they did. They are beyond despicable. They don't deserve your consideration. They don't deserve mine. I never want our child exposed to that kind of poison. It was my decision, Kelly. Do you honestly think I would allow them in any part of our lives after what they did to you?"

Tears slid down her cheeks. This hadn't been her goal. No matter how much she wanted to never be around them again, the last thing she wanted was to cause Ryan pain.

"Let's not talk about them," he said quietly. "They're no longer an issue. What I want to talk about is us. Can you ever forgive me, Kell? Can you possibly love me again?"

He rose from his perch beside her and went down the two steps to the beach below her. Then he slowly slid to his knees in front of her and reached for her hands.

"You once got on your knees and begged me to believe you. You begged me not to turn my back on you. It's my turn to beg, Kelly. I don't deserve your forgiveness. I wouldn't blame you if you *never* forgave me. But I'm begging all the same. I love you. I want us to have a life together. Here. On the island. Away from all the unhappiness of the past."

"You want us to stay here?" she whispered.

He nodded even as his hands trembled around hers. "I bought the house. I have the hospital on standby. I've made sure that our child will have the best possible care. I want us to start over, *really* start over this time. I'm begging you for that chance. Give me the chance to make you love me again."

Her heart twisted and the mind-numbing grief that had sweltered so long in her soul silently slipped away, leaving renewed hope—and love—shining in its stead. This time she didn't try to squash the hope. She let it fly.

She reached for him, framing his face, stunned

to feel the shock of tears on his cheeks. His eyes were tormented and there was desperation—fear—in his gaze, but there was also answering hope.

"I love you so very much," she said brokenly. "I've spent so long being angry, telling myself I hate you. The anger took over until I was miserable with it. It's been a constant weight pressing down on me. It's poison and I can't live this way anymore. I don't *want* to live this way anymore."

He closed his eyes and when he reopened them there was such relief and such vulnerability that she knew without a doubt that she'd made the right choice.

"If you can forgive all the hurtful, hateful things I've said to you then I can forgive you for not trusting me."

"Oh, God, Kell," he said in a wretched, pained voice. "I deserved everything you've said and more. What I did to you was unforgivable. How can you forgive me when I can't forgive myself?"

She leaned forward and kissed him, still holding his face in her hands. She stroked her hands through his hair and then over his cheeks again, smiling a tender smile all the while.

"We make quite a pair, don't we? We've made mistakes. But I like to think that we haven't given up. And that maybe we're stronger for it all. It makes me hurt that you've given up so much for me. Your family. Your friends. The city you grew up in. And you gave it up, bought a beautiful house you knew I'd love all because you loved *me.* If I don't forgive you then I'm denying myself that love and I don't want to live without you, Ryan. Or your love. Not anymore. The last months have been the worst of my life. I don't ever want to relive that kind of agony again."

He pulled her into his arms, leaning forward so they didn't tumble into the sand. He held her so tightly she couldn't breathe, but she didn't care. They were together. Finally. Without all the hurt and pain of the past. Without reservations or barriers.

As soon as she'd told him she loved him and that she forgave him it was like the weight of the world had been lifted. She felt lighter and freer than she'd ever felt. She felt…happy. Joyously, giddily happy.

"I love you so damn much, Kell," he said hoarsely. "I've always loved you. I never stopped loving you. I went to bed at night thinking about you, worrying and wondering where you were, if you were happy, if you were all right. I made all sorts of excuses for hiring someone to find you but the truth was that I couldn't live without you."

She smiled and leaned her forehead against his. "Do you think maybe we can stop beating ourselves up over things we can't change and make a pact to love each other for the rest of our lives and be happy for every day of them?"

He slid his hands over her arms, up to her neck to cup her face again. "Yeah," he breathed. "I can do that."

He pulled away, smiling, his eyes raw with emotion. "Marry me, Kell. Right away. I don't want to wait even a day. Marry me here on our beach. Just you and me and our baby."

"Our beach," she said softly. "I love the sound

of that. And yes, I'll marry you. Today, tomorrow, forever."

For the longest time they sat there on the steps leading to their beach. A beach where they'd raise their children. Where they'd laugh and love and remember how they'd pledged their love and made vows to stay together through all the trials that life threw at them.

They sat until the sun sank below the horizon and the soft colors of dusk settled over the ocean. And then when the moon rose and spilled silver over the water, Ryan carried Kelly down to the beach and they danced to the soft melody of the rolling waves.

* * * * *